WARNING

This book contains sexually explicit scenes and adult language. It may be considered offensive to some readers. This book is for sale to adults ONLY.

* * * * * * * * * * * * * * * * * *

Please store your files wisely where they cannot be accessed by underage readers.

ISBN-13: 978-1988083803
ISBN-10: 198808380X

Other books by Shyla Starr:

Persuasive Billionaire BWWM Romance Series

Stacey is trying to keep a handle on her life the best that she can. She is on the verge of losing her job and her apartment, while taking care of her sick grandmother. Her life takes an unexpected turn when she meets Charlie, who works for the construction company that is attempting to persuade her to move out of her home.

Elusive Billionaire Romance Series

Billionaire Hendrick is trying to repair his company's image by putting in some volunteer work, building a school and hospital for the impoverished children in Africa. There, he meets a beautiful African American volunteer, Jocelyn. They hit it off right away but does she belong in his world?

Lonely Billionaire Romance Series

Tricia was hired to care for billionaire John's wife, who is dying. An unlikely romance emerges after his wife, Rebecca, gives John permission to pursue his happiness after she is gone.

Ardent Billionaire Romance Series

Deirdre doesn't know what to make of the gorgeous man that seems to be interested in her. His name is Parker Walters and he seems friendly enough. There is just something off about him. Why is he trying the hide the fact that he is the heir to his father's billion dollar software empire?

Fervent Billionaire BWWM Romance Series

Alexandra had never been with a white man before. She had seen William at the café before but she always kept her distance. It was unfortunate that their first chance meeting happened when she dropped her breakfast and spilled coffee all over his expensive business suit.

Audacious Billionaire BWWM Romance Series

Chante is torn between staying close to a man beyond her league, and fleeing from him to spare herself from a hopeless position. But she finds she is propelled into a place where she needs to confront her doubts and cast her fate aside to follow the dictates of her heart. Damned if she does and miserable is she doesn't, how will Chante face the events that will lead her to a place of pure happiness or to the pits of a broken heart?

Get the latest update on new releases from the author at:

https://shylastarr.com/newsletter/

This book is Part Three of the "Tenacious Billionaire BWWM Romance Series"

Book 1 - Love Deceived

Adalia is too proud to accept help from the billionaire playboy, Trent Dawson. How long can she maintain her resolve? The bank is at her heels to repossess her business. To make matters worse, Adalia finds suspicious evidence of Trent's philandering ways. She must determine whether to trust Trent with the fate of her business and her heart.

Book 2 - Love Forgiven

Adalia is broken after a keen betrayal and the loss of her lifelong dream: her very own bakery. But she has to carry on, especially now that she's back living under her father's roof and has her semi-abusive ex-boyfriend's advances to contend with. She's determined to continue baking, even if she has to work at the local market for the rest of her days, but she can't shake thoughts of Trent and what happened between them.

Book 3 - Love Endured

Adalia Montclair is determined to be more than Mrs. Dawson. She's going to start her own catering business. But a surprise pregnancy throws a wrench in the works, in the form of her new husband himself. Trent is determined to keep Adalia safe, even if it means keeping her at home and away from her dreams, a fate she can't abide, even with a baby on board. Still, even with tension growing, Adalia can't keep her eyes or hands off her husband.

Book 4 - Love Everlasting

Adalia has just received the worst news of her entire life. Her son, Isaac, is gravely ill, and the only way to save him is a revolutionary treatment which will cost a lot of money. But a lot of money is exactly what Trent doesn't have, now that Space Inc. has gone under. Time is running out and only by working together can Adalia and Trent save their son. Their son's illness and Michelle's interference threatens to tear them apart, but Adalia isn't one to give up that easily.

Tenacious Billionaire BWWM Romance Series

Love Endured

Book Three

By Shyla Starr

Table of Contents

Chapter One

ADALIA SAT beside the infinity pool at the Grace Hotel and looked out over the deep blue ocean. Trent was inside, a quick business call to sort out his affairs before their honeymoon got into full swing.

She sighed and a smile parted her lips at the taste of salty sea air. Santorini, Greece had been her choice. The quaint white structures and sloping stairs, the city tucked against the mountain, built from the rock itself, was her idea of a fairytale.

They'd arrived a few hours ago and she itched to go out and explore, but there were matters to attend to before they could go anywhere. It irritated her that Trent took the business calls for the bakery, while she didn't have a true business of her own.

One day, she'd be the one in the expensive hotel room, making the calls, buying and selling and checking in on progress. At least, that was her dream.

"You're quiet, my love," Trent said, strolling from the cool interior and taking a seat beside her. He'd opted for an open neck cotton shirt and white pair of slacks. His tan biceps bulged to free themselves from the sleeves restraining them.

Adalia swallowed, overcome by desire again. Every day with Trent was different, an adventure, but one thing would never change – her need for him.

"How was your call?" Adalia asked, squeezing his hand in hers.

"Oh fine, fine. Just some news on the space frontier. We're going live with the IPO in a couple months, so things are going crazy."

"IPO," she repeated, wriggling her eyebrows. "You're opening the company to trade?"

"It's the next big step. We should've done it years ago. Take a look at SkyLyft. They're trading and apart from the debacle with the crash, they're doing pretty damn well." Trent scratched his chin with the tip of his index finger. "But do you really want to talk business, gorgeous?"

"I want to do many things. Including you," she quipped.

He chuckled and picked up a bottle of champagne from the poolside table. He poured for both of them, then handed her one.

"I think we're overdue for a toast after all the shit we've been through," Trent said, then clinked the rim of his glass against hers.

"I couldn't agree more." She raised the flute to her lips. Nausea bubbled in her stomach and she pulled it away again.

"What's wrong?"

"Nothing… I just feel a little strange. I'm fine, really, don't worry." It was probably the plane food. They'd served some kind of exotic Indian dish and it hadn't gone down well.

Trent slid his arm around her shoulders and pulled her close. He leaned his head against hers and they looked out over the ocean together. "I couldn't have chosen a better destination myself."

"Oh please, you would've had us hiking in Machu Picchu," she said, then pressed a hand to her stomach. Man, the last thing she needed was to start their honeymoon going down on the toilet. That would almost be as bad as DeShawn's attempt to discredit her at the wedding.

Trent's eyes glistened in the morning light. He tipped his head back and soaked up the sun.

Bile crept up Adalia's throat and she stood abruptly.

"What's wrong?" Trent rose immediately and stroked his fingers down her spine.

"I don't know. I just don't feel well." She managed to stand before the nausea completely overwhelmed her. She slapped her palm across her mouth, turned and sprinted for their room. She crashed through into the pristine white suite and grimaced at the off chance she'd let loose before she hit the bathroom.

Adalia skidded around the corner and slid into the bathroom. She didn't have time to close the door. She

crouched over the toilet and let breakfast, dinner and
what had to be every meal she'd ever eaten present
itself in reverse order.

"Oh god, Adalia," Trent hurried into the bathroom
and stroked her back. "It's okay, I'm here."

She didn't have the strength to wave him away. So
much for romance on their honeymoon. She spent
another two minutes in the same state, then flushed the
toilet and collapsed against the wall.

Why was everything white in this damn place?

Trent handed her a couple squares of toilet paper
and she dabbed at the corners of her mouth. "I'm
sorry," she mumbled, "I didn't expect that to happen."

"Don't say sorry, Adalia. It's not like you can help
it. I'm worried about you… this looks like food
poisoning. We should go see a doctor." He cupped her
cheek in his palm and tilted his head to the side, bright
blue eyes brimming with concern.

Adalia could barely lift her head. She was
exhausted and sweaty, and God, she just wanted a glass
of water and a good sleep.

"Don't be ridic –" She pushed him back and
vomited noisily into the toilet again. Where could all
this have come from –? She'd surely puked out
everything else.

"That's it. We're going to see a doctor." Trent rose
and hurried into the living room.

Adalia flushed again and struggled into the standing position, then shuffled to the sink. She grasped her cheeks and slapped them to take away the numbness. What the hell was this?

She'd read an article once about eating yogurt to get the local bacteria when visiting a new country, but this was insane. She'd hardly had a chance to unpack. Hell, she'd eaten nothing since they'd arrived, not even a sip of damned champagne.

Adalia brushed her teeth, then washed her mouth out and gargled. That would have to do for now – there was no helping the clammy hands and weak knees.

Trent appeared in the doorway. "Are you done?"

"Yeah, I'm okay. Trent, we really don't need to go to the doctor. It's just a bug… it will pass."

"Like hell it will. Let's go. There's a doctor just around the corner." He guided her from the bathroom with a smile and a gentle caress in the small of her back.

***

Dr. Michelakis had a moustache to rival Yosemite Sam, and deep brown eyes which expressed a lot of sympathy. He tugged on one of the face caterpillars and leaned forward.

"What's the problem?" he asked, in his thick Greek accent.

Adalia leaned back in the plastic chair at the front of his desk and laid her hands over her belly. "I've got a tummy bug or something. I keep throwing up and I feel a bit sweaty and weak."

The good doctor squeaked back in his chair and studied her, gaze sweeping over her belly and then to Trent.

"Alright. We take urine and blood sample, then we check to see the problem."

"How long will it take until we know what's wrong?" Trent asked, grasping Adalia's knee and running his thumb along the outside of her thigh.

"Maybe hour or two. Our lab is empty of samples now, so should go very, very quickly." Dr. Michelakis rose and walked to the door. He opened it and shouted something in Greek, then walked back to his desk. "Nurse is coming now to take your blood sample." He slapped a plastic receptacle onto the table and smiled at Adalia. "You make a pee in this one now."

What a charmer. She nodded to him and snatched up the plastic container, then hurried out of the room and to the restroom across the hall. Five minutes later, she was back in his office with a vial of yellow fluid. A nurse was waiting, holding a needle and a syringe.

"Is this really necessary?" she asked. "It's just the flu or stomach bug."

"Just let the nurse do what she has to do, Adalia," Trent advised.

She shot him a venomous look. He wasn't the one who had to get holes poked in him by a trigger happy Greek nurse with a nose that could've climbed trees.

The bloodletting was done in another fifteen minutes and Adalia settled in to wait. They'd decided to hang around in the doctor's office. Actually, Trent had decided they weren't going anywhere until they knew what was wrong with her and how to fix it.

"You're blowing this out of proportion," she grunted. "So what if I have food poisoning? I'll throw up a couple times and stay in bed for a day or two. It's not a big deal."

"Of course it's a big deal," he snapped, "I want you to enjoy our honeymoon, not be confined to the bedroom. At least not under this pretext. God, Adalia. Don't you care about your own health?"

"Don't start on me, I'm not in the mood," she said.

The office was empty. The doctor had popped out to catch a quick lunch. Apparently, things moved slowly in Santorini, and his afternoon was clear except for the blood and urine tests.

She grabbed the bottle of water Trent had bought for her and unscrewed the cap. She swigged a few gulps then pulled a face at the resurgence of nausea.

"What is it? Do you need to go to the bathroom? Are you going to throw up again?" he rattled off the questions in rapid succession.

"Oh my God!" Adalia slammed the bottle onto the table top. "Would you fucking relax? You're starting to get on my nerves now."

"I'm just looking out for you," he said, his tone turning sullen. He looked out the window and silence fell between them.

Oh well, it was better than constant questions and concerns. She'd never seen him this way before. He was terrified for her safety, yet there was nothing seriously wrong with her. Trent had revealed a different side to himself, a more vulnerable side. Maybe if she hadn't been about to toss her cookies all over the desk, she would have found it endearing.

The door cracked open behind them and Trent straightened and turned. Adalia stared dead ahead, seething for God alone knew what reason. Because Trent cared enough to rush her to a doctor? That was a good trait, so why did it piss her off this much?

"Ah good, you still here." Dr. Michelakis entered and bustled to his desk, carrying a brown folder and a moustache coated in bread crumbs. He took a seat and brushed the remains of his lunch away from his lips.

"So, what's the verdict?" Trent asked, before Adalia could say a word.

"Yes, what's wrong with me?" Adalia followed up, casting another expression of irritation at her husband. What a way to spend their first day as a married couple.

"Is very simple. I look at the urine sample first and find out the result, but want to confirm with blood test." The doctor opened the file and slid two pieces of paper onto his desk. He positioned his elbows on the wood surface, balled up his fists and pressed them into his cheeks while studying the results.

"And that means what?" Adalia tapped her foot impatiently. She wanted to get home and nap as soon as possible.

"It means what I suspected. You are going to have a baby." He spread his arms wide, then made a cradle and rocked it from side to side. "Congratulations. Such a lovely surprise."

"What?!" Adalia spat. "You're kidding, right? I'm pregnant? I'm getting sick because I'm pregnant. Is this some kind of joke?"

"No joke. You no worry, this is good news for you. Good news about little baby." Dr. Michelakis stood and gestured to the door.

Adalia couldn't bring herself to stand. "I'm pregnant."

"Yes, now have good afternoon. You take the vitamins." He scratched out a prescription on a piece of paper and handed it to Trent. He accepted it, expression completely blank.

Adalia's mind was a mess of emotions and thoughts. How was this possible?

She didn't look at Trent all the way to the drug store. They got back to the hotel and she walked into the bedroom and closed the door, then climbed right into bed, gripping her stomach.

Chapter Two

"Are we going to talk about this?" Trent stood in the doorway, with his one hand on the handle and the other on his hip.

"No?" She pulled the covers over her head and sighed.

"Why not?"

"I believe that's classed as 'talking about it'." Adalia grasped her stomach and lay on her side, breathing through her nose. She wasn't unhappy about the baby. In fact, she was pretty darn happy to be carrying Trent's child. She was just in shock. And she was afraid of what he'd say about this.

"Adalia," he began, then paused and walked to the bed. He sat down on the edge and stroked her through the thin duvet. "Adalia, I love you and I just want you to know I'm really happy about this. I know it's a big deal, but it's not like we can't afford to have a child."

She poked her head out like a prairie dog, and beamed at him. "I'm really happy too. Sorry I distanced myself. I'm just… I just was in shock. That's all… afraid."

"Afraid of what?"

"Things are going to change now. Good change and maybe some bad change too." She pressed her lips together and eased herself into a sitting position. Her stomach burbled a complaint.

"Bad change," Trent repeated, "I don't know about that."

"I'm not the kind of woman who gets a nanny. I want to raise my child myself, with you, obviously, but if I do that, it means giving up on a few dreams."

"Adalia, you have everything you could possibly want. A husband, a home, a successful bakery…" he said.

"That's not mine, it's yours." It slipped out before she could stop it. Not that she'd want to stop it. The truth was the truth and she didn't like hiding from it.

"What are you talking about? We set up that bakery together." He clenched his fists, but didn't shift closer to her. "Why would you even say that?"

"Trent, don't even pretend that I have as much to do with that bakery as you do."

"I'm getting sick of this. You're talking crazy." He stood and walked to the window, staring out at Santorini.

Adalia sighed and sat up slowly. "I didn't dream of owning another bakery. I'm done with that. I dreamed of my own catering business. Independence has always been my dream too."

"What do you need independence for when you have me." He didn't phrase it as a question, but more of a challenge.

"Get real. Everyone needs independence. At least on some level," Adalia murmured. She let the sheets fall back and looked at his strong back, the stubborn set of his shoulders. "I want financial independence."

"This is what's on your mind right now? We've got a baby on the way. Your focus should be there… not on some dream catering business," Trent snapped.

She started as if he'd struck her and got out of bed a second later. "Don't you talk to me like that! I'll do whatever it takes to support our child in every way, but don't expect me to give up on my dreams. Just because I'm going to be a mother, doesn't mean I stop being a woman, or a businesswoman for that matter."

"A businesswoman. Adalia, need I remind you about the untimely end to your first bakery?" Trent turned from the window, gaze aflame with rage.

"Thanks for that." Adalia walked to the door and let herself out of the bedroom, then plonked down on the white living room chair. It was good to know that her husband had faith in her skills as a business person.

"I'm sorry," Trent said, standing in the doorway, "I don't know what came over me. I just can't stand the thought of you overworking yourself or not relying on me for a change."

"Who do you think you married? You don't know me if you think I'll give up on this. I told you from the start that I don't take handouts." She was too angry to see straight. She massaged her stomach to still the nausea. It rose again despite her efforts.

"I don't expect you to take handouts, but I do expect you not to overdo it when you're carrying our unborn child."

"God, we're on unborn children speeches about a half hour after we found out I'm carrying. This is insane, Trent. Just calm down and hear what I'm saying to you. All I'm asking for is a little moral support."

"You have support. That's what *I'm* saying to *you*." Trent patted her on the back of the hand. "Now, can we please put this behind us and move on with your vacation?"

She opened her mouth to tell him that there wasn't a chance in hell they could put it behind them, but all that came out was a burp. She launched herself off the sofa and dashed for the bathroom again, fighting the nausea every step of the way.

Adalia lost that battle the minute she got into the bathroom.

She emerged twenty minutes later to find Trent packing their bags in the master bedroom.

"What are you doing?"

"I'm taking us home. You'll be more comfortable back at the house." He took out one of the special numbers she'd bought for the honeymoon, folded it carefully and placed it in her bag.

"So that's it. Our honeymoon's over? Just like that, you've made the decision because I threw up a few times."

Trent stopped packing and came over to her. He wrapped his arms around her waist and pulled her against his chest. "I just want to do what's best for us, what's best for you and the baby. Right now, that means getting us home safely. Besides, we'll have just as much fun as we would've had here." He planted a sloppy kiss on her forehead then returned to packing.

Apparently, the issue was no longer up for debate.

***

The air hostess, a woman in a blue suit with her silky smooth dark hair pinned back in a bun, stood beside Adalia's seat, wearing the smile of a person practiced in patience. "Yes, ma'am, we have fish available, but all our meals are pre-prepared. I can't have a specific dish made up for you."

"She's pregnant," Trent put in, "this is probably one of her cravings."

Adalia ignored her husband and grasped the bag of peanuts. "So, that's a no on the Norwegian salmon?" She wasn't unreasonable – didn't expect the air hostess to magic it out of thin air. She'd just expected a little variety in first class.

The thought of anything but Norwegian salmon made her sick to the stomach.

"I'm sorry, ma'am. We are serving hake this evening, however. Should I bring you some of that?"

"No, thank you. Just a glass of water." *And possibly a pain killer*. A headache had set in soon after they'd arrived at the airport.

The air hostess smiled amicably and sauntered off up the aisle, touching the seats and the arms of passengers as she went, exchanging a word here and there.

Adalia rubbed at her nose. She could smell everything at the moment, including the DKNY which the lady across from her had chosen to spritz on by the gallon.

She was irritable, though it probably wasn't from the hormones yet. The doctor had said she was only 4 weeks, right before they'd left his office.

"Do you want to talk about what happened earlier?" Trent brushed his fingertips up her arm, leaving a wake of goose flesh.

"Not really. I'm tired and grumpy… I don't want to take it out on you," Adalia replied. That was probably a more mature reaction than dashing through their vacation suite and hiding under the Egyptian cotton.

Trent nodded and went quiet for a few moments. He shifted then said, "I want you to take it easy when we get home. I'll handle the business for the bakery."

"Oh please," she replied. "It's not like I have a dreaded disease or something. I can still function in everyday life. I'm not even far along yet. You're seriously blowing this out of proportion. I thought it was sweet at first, but yeah, it's starting to irritate me now."

"I want you to have a good pregnancy. I want you to be happy," he said.

"Then let me do what I have to do, instead of trying to restrict me." Adalia paused and studied him, relishing the sight of his strong jaw and nose, before continuing. "I need freedom to be happy. I don't know what type of woman you're used to, but I'm certainly not the kind to take orders from a man."

"Stop it," Trent said, grabbing her hand and raising it to his lips. He brushed a trail of hot kisses over her knuckles and up to the inside of her elbow. That was his signature move – it drove her wild.

Heat flooded Adalia's core, quickly replaced by a wave of nausea. "I told you I don't want to talk about this."

"I don't want to fight." Trent squeezed her hand gently. "I'm only being protective."

"I know that." But there wasn't anything else to say. The fact remained that she would pursue her dreams and be a successful mother, or at least she'd try her heart out. She had to establish independence somehow, prove herself as she'd always wanted.

Her child wouldn't respect her if she was some kept woman. Trent's billionaire wife, lucky enough to marry a rich man. She glanced around the cabin and chewed her bottom lip. First class flights paid for by Mr. Dawson.

Why did she find it offensive that he'd paid for her? It seemed unreasonable on her part, but –

The hostess walked past with the food trolley, heading towards the back of the plane, carrying dish upon dish of hake and potato wedges, beef sliders and green beans. The odor of cooked food travelled throughout the cabin.

"Smells good," Trent said. He craned his neck at the approaching hostess, licking his lips. They hadn't had a bite since they arrived in Santorini that morning.

That smell would've brought out the hunger in a normal person. The scent of grilled meat and white fish was too much to bear for her. Adalia pressed her lips together and denied the bile rising in her throat. Not now, oh God, please not now.

"Adalia?" He leaned forward, all sympathy and sweetness. "Do you want me to get you a bucket?"

A bucket. She coughed out a laugh and stood abruptly, then hurried down the aisle towards the bathrooms at the back of the plane. Businessmen in suits and ties stared at her as she hurried past, women wearing gold necklaces and massive diamond rings raised their eyebrows in disdain.

These were not her kind of people. White and upper class, probably swimming in money from the moment of conception. They stared at her like she was an outsider. She sprinted past them all, secretly enjoying the shock which registered on their faces, then rammed her way into the cubicle.

She dropped to her knees and slammed the door shut with the heel of her shoe. Adalia dry heaved for about five minutes, but her stomach was empty except for a dribble of water. She coughed, stood and washed her mouth out anyway.

The door handle rattled. "Adalia?" Trent murmured from the other side of the door. "Are you alright, my love?"

"Sure, I'm fine," she said, staring at her reflection in the mirror, the fleshy cheeks and full lips. She massaged her stomach then dropped her hands to cradle her womb. There wasn't a bump yet, but for a moment she imagined the tiny flutter of movement within.

"I'll be out in a minute," she said.

Trent's receding footsteps did nothing to comfort her.

Chapter Three

"Well, that was the worst flight ever," she remarked, as they traversed the white stairs from the plane to the runway below. She'd run back and forth at least five times and managed two mouthfuls of food, total. Of course, she'd brought it all up again.

"Don't worry, we'll be home soon and I'll get you some anti-nausea meds. You can put your feet up and watch the Daily Show with Trevor Noah." Trent guided her by the small of her back, and placed a gentle kiss on her neck.

"Thanks, gorgeous," she whispered, "I'm sorry I've been such a nightmare."

"You'll feel way better once we get to our place." Trent slid his arm around her hips and held her loosely. He was so considerate, conscious of the fact that she didn't feel good, and it made her want to ravage him, nausea aside.

They hit the runway and strolled along, hand in hand, talking amiably for the first time in two days. It was good to get back to some level of normality, though technically their relationship had been anything but normal.

They got to the conveyor, collected their bags and made their way out of the airport. A row of taxis waited out front, idling for people who didn't have transportation or family members and friends to pick them up.

Trent led her past the yellow cars and out into the parking lot. A row of limousines waited beyond the taxis, and several of the passengers from first class stood beside them, watching as chauffeurs loaded their luggage into the respective trunks.

"This one's ours," Trent said, pointing it out. He strode powerfully towards it, carrying both their bags in one hand.

The back door of the limo opened and a sleek white leg ending in a black stiletto slid from it and hit the pavement. Michelle Van Heerden stepped from its leather-entombed depths, stinking of Coco Chanel and privilege.

"Mr. Dawson," she simpered, fanning herself then sweeping a few strands of blonde hair behind her ear. "Welcome to Hades."

"The temperature has climbed in, what, a day?" He laughed and the hair on the back of Adalia's neck stood on end, driven by jealousy. Why was Michelle Van Heerden everywhere they went? It was like living in Legally Blonde.

"I didn't expect you back so soon. Was the accommodation not to your liking?" Michelle looked

Adalia up and down, insinuating what she meant by 'accommodation' with her eyes.

"Everything was perfect, thank you," Trent replied.

"What are you doing here?" Adalia snapped, finally growing tired of chewing on the side of her tongue. She tasted iron and swallowed hard.

Michelle turned to her slowly, wearing a shit-eating grin. "Oh, Miss Montclair, I didn't see you there," she murmured, "as impossible as that may seem."

"Excuse me?" Adalia glared at Trent's runway model of an assistant.

"Oh, just a joke. You've got such a large… character." Michelle's lips parted even wider.

"Oh, not that," Adalia replied, letting a smile of her own slip to the surface. "You called me Miss Montclair. I'm Mrs. Dawson now. I suggest you address me that way. Now, kindly get the bags and put them in the trunk."

Michelle took a step back as if she'd been physically accosted.

"What are you doing here, Michelle?" Trent asked, placing their luggage on the ground. He dusted his hands off and wrapped them around Adalia's shoulders, nuzzling her neck with the tip of his nose.

"I came to talk about the impending release of our IPO."

"The company's IPO," he corrected her. He straightened and arranged his cotton shirt, upper lip curling slightly.

Adalia chuckled to herself – the man was obsessed with suits, the casual wear had to be killing him, especially now that his assistant was here, talking business. That was her excuse at least. Adalia wasn't fooled. Michelle had set her sights on Trent long ago; the fact that Adalia had married him had to be the worst torture for the spoiled bitch.

Trent wiggled his head from side to side in an uncharacteristic motion of indecision. "I'd much rather settle in and meet you at the office about this. Have we heard from –?"

"Withnail Harrington? Yes, yes we have. He's determined to buy up most of the public shares once we go live." Michelle folded her arms beneath her breasts to display what she thought of that. The tight red blouse and tighter black skirt did her body plenty of favors.

"And have there been any messages for me?" Trent let go of Adalia, his focus solely on his assistant now.

"Plenty, you'd think you were gone for more than just a *day*." Michelle examined her lurid pink fingernails then ran her thumbnail over the hem of her shirt. "I'll get us back to the office."

"No, we're going home first to drop Adalia off. She needs her rest." Trent opened the door for his wife.

"Yes, I'm sure she does. Long trip, right?" Michelle reluctantly retrieved the bags and popped the trunk. She shoved them in and slammed it shut.

"Yeah. We've got wonderful news out of it though," Trent said, extending a hand to Adalia.

She took it, brushing her fingers across his palm, picturing his hands on her breasts, neck, shoulders. Adalia was heat and desire for a moment again, lost in his touch and the gentle declaration of love in his gaze.

"Oh? What's the good news, Trent?" Michelle watched from beside the limo, the noon day sun reflecting off her bleach blonde hair, absorbed by her perfectly tanned skin – someone had hit the tanning booth.

Trent looked at Adalia and smiled, then nodded proudly for her to relay the news.

She met Michelle's gaze. "I'm pregnant."

The assistant's face fell into disbelief, the feigned adoration and respect was sucked into the stratosphere.

Adalia chuckled all the way into the limo and settled back into the leather seat. So, perhaps the honeymoon hadn't ended on that much of a sour note after all.

***

Sylvester Montclair stood on the porch, watching as Adalia walked up the cracked sidewalk. She met her father's gaze and smiled warmly, even though they'd parted on rocky terms.

Sylvester stretched and scratched his neck. "Didn't expect you to come around any time soon."

"I know you're not a fan of Trent, Dad, but it wouldn't hurt to call once in a while," she replied. She strode up the front stairs and stood in front of him.

Even in his old age, with grey in his hair and watery eyes, he towered over her. He'd finally overcome the vicious bout of flu which had taken him down for two entire months. He was larger than life, her dad, and even though they'd had their differences, she held nothing but respect for him.

"How's business?" Adalia asked.

"Business, business," he repeated, shaking his head, "that's always the first thing on your tongue, girl. I'm fine by the way. Come on in and make us some coffee. I wasn't expecting company."

He turned and marched into the house, the shuffling gait and blanket absent.

Adalia shook visions of her ill father from her mind, and focussed on the old commanding one. The one she'd grown up with, not the frail man who'd kicked her out of his life because she'd chosen Trent.

She followed him inside, walking through the entrance hall, past the door to her old bedroom toward the kitchen. She hurried to take the cups from her father's hands and placed them on the counter. She fished around in the cupboard for the coffee and a filter and brought out a teaspoon and the sugar. Adalia made the coffee as she would have normally if she had still stayed there.

***

"How are you?" Adalia asked, now that enough time had passed to make the question genuine again.

"I'm fine. Healthy as a horse, back on track. Even got me a date tonight." He grinned and accepted the hot cup of coffee.

Adalia poured what was left of the coffee into her cup – just enough so she wouldn't have to make more – and stirred it lazily. "That's great, Dad. I'm really happy for you." How would she even begin to broach the topic of the baby with him? God, he still didn't trust Trent after all this time. What if he rejected his grandbaby?

She licked her lips nervously. "And how's the business?"

"Going good… just fine really. Making enough to pay the bills and a little extra. Saving it for a rainy day, though I don't know what kind, since I don't plan on retiring any time soon."

That was her dad, always working.

Adalia drank her coffee then froze. Was she allowed coffee? How would this affect the fetus?

"What's the matter?" Sylvester asked, frowning above the rim of his mug.

"Nothing, I'm fine," she murmured, and carefully placed the coffee to one side where she wouldn't be tempted.

"How's business going with you, girl? That why you came back from your honeymoon so early?" He drank deeply from his mug, finished the contents and placed it in the bottom of the sink with a *clink*.

"Business is… well, the bakery is fine. My business isn't going yet," she murmured, then dragged her teeth over her bottom lip. "That's not technically why we came back so early."

"Then why?"

"I got real sick, Dad," she said, rubbing her stomach.

Sylvester narrowed his eyes. "You seem fine to me? What kinda sick are we talking here?"

"The kind that ends in nine months." Adalia wasn't sure how long morning sickness lasted, but the hint worked for her purposes.

"What?!" He covered his mouth with a trembling hand. "You can't be serious."

"I'm as serious as a positive test. I'm pregnant, Dad." She smiled at him, the quavering kind which signified her uncertainty.

"Well, damn," he replied, "I mean shit. I mean, well that's great, girl. Congratulations." He opened his arms for a hug and she rushed into them, finally connecting with her father after what seemed like an eternity of disagreements and disapproval.

"Thanks," she said, pulling away after a good two minutes.

"I'm serious, I'm real happy for you. And it's Trent who's the – uh –" he broke off and waved in the general direction of her stomach.

"Of course. He's my husband and the father of my child."

"Oh okay, well, that's good I guess," Sylvester replied, then clapped his hands and rubbed them together. "I won't pretend that I have any love for the man, or any trust either, but I'm willing to give him the benefit of the doubt, especially now he's going to be the father of my grandson. Or granddaughter," he put in, quickly. Sylvester Montclair actually gave a gleeful cackle.

"I thought you should know and hoped you'd be a part of the baby's life." Adalia brushed her hair back, regaining a small measure of composure. Outside the window, birds chirped and cars hummed in the streets. A group of kids were kicking a ball down the sidewalk, laughing and kidding around.

"Anything else bothering you?" Sylvester had always known how to cut to the heart of things.

"Business. Or rather, the lack thereof." She leaned back against the counter. Her dad went to get her a chair but stopped when she waved him off.

"I thought the bakery was doing good."

"It's doing fine, but you know that's not really my business, Dad. I want something of my own."

"The catering?" Sylvester asked then nodded to himself. "You can still do that. Even with a baby, you can still do that. Take it from a parent who worked and raised kids."

"Trent doesn't want me to overdo it. He's afraid I'll overexert myself and hurt the baby." She felt like a traitor for admitting it, but she needed her father to tell her what she wanted to hear.

Sylvester leaned in and grabbed her by the shoulders. "You listen carefully now, girl. If you have a dream, you go after it, no matter what. You hear me?"

"Yes, Dad."

Chapter Four

Adalia pulled up to the house in a Mercedes SLK55 AMG. Trent had bought it for her as a wedding gift. It reeked of luxury and leather, not something she was accustomed to, having come from a humble background. A Mercedes? Hell, she could barely afford a broken down Ford with her own money, and now she had this.

She checked her reflection in the mirror and grimaced. *Nice hair, Adalia. Cowlicks are totally in this season.* She patted at the offending section until it flattened, then took out her lip gloss and applied a fine, cherry-flavored layer. *That'll do the trick.*

The house was lit by external floodlights, highlighting the white walls, including alcoves with potted plants. Yet most of the lights indoors were off, except for the study light and the bedroom.

Trent was in one of those rooms, waiting for her... or maybe not. Maybe he was still out with that bitch of an assistant, going over the files on the impending IPO release.

Adalia pattered her nails against her palms then grasped the smooth door handle and let herself out of the car. "No sense delaying it," she murmured. She'd have to talk to Trent about this again.

She flapped the front of her blouse and stuck out her tongue. And she was in serious need of a shower. The flight hadn't done her any favors… neither had the unseasonable heat this time of year.

Adalia shut the car door and paced towards the house, breathing in the thick summer air, the warmth seeping from the stones paving the drive. She reached the bottom of the stairs, just as the front door swung open.

Michelle stepped out, dusting off her tight pencil skirt with a soft smile. "Miss Montclair, what a pleasure."

"Mrs. Dawson." She didn't return the smile. Maybe that made her petty, but so what. Michelle's attempts to upset her were blatant, that smile was far from friendly.

"Right, right, married now," she murmured, "and pregnant too. I wonder what that will be like."

"Huh?" Adalia asked, in her best 'bitch, I don't have time for you' tone.

"You're already that size. I can't imagine what you'll look like at nine months." Michelle's smile disappeared and she dry washed her hands then flapped them in mid-air.

"Get off my front porch," Adalia replied. She kept her arms at her sides and her jaw loose, relaxed, but inside, God, inside she was an inferno. Van Heerden had pushed and pushed from the start, toe over the line here, downright disrespect there.

Michelle stood her ground, glaring down at Adalia from the top of the stairs.

"I told you to get off my front porch." She folded her fingers into her palm and formed a fist. "Now."

Michelle tittered a laugh. "Or what?" She flopped her hands around in mock placation. "No, no, never mind. I'm leaving anyway. I've just finished off Trent, now I've got to get back to the office and get back to work. Some of us actually earn our way in this world."

That was a lot of venom distilled into a single sentence. Adalia jammed her jaw shut and waited.

"Aren't you going to say anything? No snarky reply to put me in my place, Miss Montclair?" Michelle carried on poking the sleeping bear.

No, this bear wasn't asleep. She was wide awake, biding her time until the perfect moment presented itself.

Adalia took the stairs slowly, one at a time, never breaking eye contact with the blonde assistant. She reached the top step and walked on, past Van Heerden towards the front door of the mansion. This was her home now.

Michelle burst into laughter behind her, a sour noise which swam down the back of Adalia's spine. Footsteps followed and the assistant swung into view, blocking her path into the house.

"You think you've won, don't you? Big black bitch gets what she wants at last." Michelle threw back her head and forced laughter at the eaves. She cut off abruptly and stepped up to Adalia, face crumpling and a muscle twitching below her eyes. "But you don't get it. You'll never win. You will pay for this and Trent will too."

"You stay the fuck away from Trent," Adalia hissed, then jammed her mouth shut. So much for keeping her cool.

Michelle's eyes glistened and she raised her head. She glanced into the depths of the mansion, past the marble hallway and up the stairs to the bedroom. "I've been in there before, never forget that. Trent Dawson wasn't always yours, Adalia, and he won't be yours forever."

She turned and marched off, swaying her hips, unstoppable in her four inch heels.

Thunder rumbled in the distance. The first of the summer storms had come. Adalia looked to the shrouded sky – the clouds had rolled in during that pleasant little encounter – and cursed the day she'd met that woman.

"Adalia?" Trent's footsteps rang on the marble as he walked out of the study. He halted in the doorway. "Come on, baby, come inside before the storm breaks. You'll get soaked."

She stared at him for a moment, drinking in his details and everything which had passed between them.

Their relationship had been agony to start with. She'd resisted him with all her might, but the love they shared had won out.

"Adalia," Trent said, tone edgy and eyes furrowing at the corners. "You'll catch a cold out there." He held out a hand to her and she took it, spurred on by his masculinity. He closed the distance between them and kissed her cheek, raising the hairs on her arms. "Let's go to bed."

Adalia walked into their home without sparing a backward glance for Michelle Van Heerden.

***

"Do you want to grab a bite to eat before we go upstairs?" Trent asked, glancing at her stomach as if he had x-ray vision and could see that kid growing in there.

"No, I don't feel great. Think I should just get some rest," she replied, gritting her teeth. God, she loved him like crazy, yet he knew just what to do to irritate the living shit out of her. She wasn't just his darling Adalia anymore, voluptuous and ambitious as he'd put it. She was the baby carrier.

She was reduced to 'mom' before she'd even become a mom. And it didn't feel sexy or empowering, because she hadn't gotten more than a few minutes to think about her unborn child, not even a long bath to lie there and connect with the baby… hell, with the concept of a baby.

"Adalia, you have to eat something," Trent said, after a long silence. He held her hand tight and wore a smile which was tighter.

"Don't start with me." Adalia wormed out of his grip and strode towards the stair case.

"Stop," Trent commanded.

She froze at the tone and a red wave flooded her vision. How dare he speak to her like this?

"Let's get something clear here. I am not yours to command and I never have been," Adalia replied, turning slowly to face him. She took a measured step forward then stopped, staring into his eyes.

"You are when you're carrying my child in your womb," he snapped then drew in a sharp breath. "Adalia, I'm sorry, I didn't meant that. It just –"

"Just what? Slipped out? You don't own me, Trent. I'm your wife, not your possession and if I'd known you'd start behaving like this after the wedding, I wouldn't have become that."

"Don't say that," he said, pacing sideways then back again. He pinched his lips together like he had to stop himself from saying whatever the hell he wanted to say.

"I'll say whatever I want." Adalia crossed her arms. The lights in the hall highlighted the lightened streaks in Trent's hair and the two day old stubble raking up his neck and along his jawline.

She inhaled through her nose and let out a long stream of tension through her mouth.

"You'll never understand how I feel about this," she said.

"Ditto."

"Alright, then what's the point in talking about it. I'm going to bed." She clipped the sentences short and made for the stairs. She marched up the first three, holding her head high. She was right about this… he couldn't make her into what he wanted.

"Adalia, just stop. Please, talk to me about this." His voice dropped lower and bled tension.

"We've talked about it at least two times since I told you I was pregnant and you still don't get it. Now, it's not about the fact that you're turning me into your kept woman… it's about you. Again!" She threw her hands up in the air, grasping the railing of the stairs, and turning back.

"Me?" Trent spluttered for a few minutes, then collected himself and smoothed his hair back. "Since when is it ever about me?"

"It's always about you. Mr. Billionaire. You forced me into a bakery with you; you hunted me down and got me; you wanted Michelle to stay on, so she's still around making shit comments whenever she sees me."

"Shit comments?" His gaze clouded, lips curling in distaste.

"That's not the point right now." Adalia ran a hand over her hair and sighed. "You got all that and now you want me to be nothing but 'wife' and 'mom'. You can't have my identity, Trent, you can't have that too."

"God, I can't believe you feel this way," he murmured. He took a step towards her then stopped. "How long?" he asked, in a whisper weighed down by emotion.

"How long what?"

"How long have you felt this way?" Trent's arms hung at his sides, the sleeves of his cotton shirt were rolled back to expose his forearms, which were corded with muscle.

"And here we go again. All about Trent. This is the Trent show. Your feelings are hurt and we're going to talk about it right now. But I'm frustrated because you want to own me and the subject changes," she spat.

"I don't want to own you. I just want to keep you and the baby safe."

"And safe entails keeping me from my dream? I'm telling you, I want my own catering business and nothing is going to keep me from doing that." She made her fists tight, and her fingernails bit into her palm, leaving half-moon imprints.

Trent swore under his breath. "I'm not trying to keep you from anything."

"That's good," she said, "because you wouldn't succeed even if you tried." She turned and strode up the stairs. She wanted a bath, distance from Trent and a moment, just a damn moment, to relax and focus on what was about to happen to her body and their lives.

There was a baby in her womb, his baby, their baby, and she wanted to be the best woman and mother she could be. She couldn't do that if she became a rich housewife, a person without the burning desire to succeed.

If she had a girl, would she really want the baby to learn from that kind of example? And how could a little boy learn to respect women, when she knuckled under every time Trent told her to?

Adalia shook her hair back and went to the bathroom, then locked herself in, taking solace in the white tiled walls and the small potted plant in the corner. She turned on the taps and waited until the room filled with steam, then cloaked herself in the warmth of water, slopping it onto the floor without a care.

She *would* be a success. For herself, for her child and for Trent too.

Chapter Five

Adalia stepped into their bedroom, holding the towel to her chest, shoulders up because frankly, she didn't want to talk anymore.

Trent sat on the edge of the bed with his shirt unbuttoned, revealing those rock hard abs. "I'm sorry," he said immediately. "I don't want you to feel that way."

She chewed her bottom lip. "That's okay." It wasn't truly okay, but she did love him more than words could express. She wanted to be there for him, she wanted to have his baby, all of it.

"Adalia," he said, rising and stripping off his shirt. He wadded it into a ball and shot it into the corner. "I love you and I don't own you, I know that. I –"

She dropped the towel and he cut off mid-sentence. "I'm tired of talking," she murmured.

Adalia walked to the dresser and opened it, rooting around inside for a night shirt. She bent slightly, presenting herself to him.

He groaned. "You're teasing me."

"Glad you noticed," she replied, wiggling her ass. "Consider it a punishment." Cool air fanned her folds and her flesh prickled.

Trent walked up behind her and ran a finger along her ass cheek, trailing it down and around to rest it at her entrance. "You're not angry?"

How was she supposed to answer that with his finger on her pussy, waiting to penetrate her? Desire flooded in her core and she was instantly wet.

"Are you angry?" Trent asked, tracing her folds, her quivering, slick hole. He inserted his forefinger an inch.

She cried out softly. "No."

"Good," he replied, his breath hitched in his chest, then feathered across her skin.

Adalia was a little angry that he thought he could control her and take her whenever he wanted. Trent was a powerful man. He hadn't married her for being weak, so how could he expect her to do anything but argue for what she wanted?

He plunged his fingers into her, stroking her G-spot, urging her to come for him. Her pussy clenched tight and her eyes rolled back in her head.

She wouldn't climax yet. Adalia turned and placed her hand flat on his chest. "Nuh-uh, it's my turn."

"Wh-what?" That was the first time he'd ever stammered.

"That's right." Adalia licked her lips then grinned. She walked him backwards and the backs of his calves hit the base of the bed.

Trent sat down heavily and stared up at her. "What do you think you're doing?" His voice was heavy with desire, urging her to give him exactly what he needed and what she wanted from him. "You're looking for trouble."

"Shut up," she said, grabbing his chin. She pressed her lips to his and kissed him, swiping her tongue across his and forcing it deep into his mouth.

He responded with a tight groan.

Adalia pecked a line of kisses down his chin, then opened her mouth and sucked on his neck. She licked her way down his chest and grasped at his sides.

He was tense, staring up at her with wild desire in his eyes, his mouth half-open.

Adalia reached down and unzipped his pants, then brought out his massive cock. He was painfully hard for her, already dripping pre-cum. She kneeled between his legs and dragged his pants down to his ankles.

"Adalia," he whispered.

"Quiet," she replied then she licked the tip of his dick. She sucked up his juices and circled his head with her tongue.

Trent growled and threw his head back, grasping her hair and guiding her gently.

Their honeymoon had been nothing like this. She'd needed him so bad, from the minute they'd met until now, and yet opportunities had rarely presented themselves.

Adalia sucked his head slowly then ran her fingers up the inside of his thighs, scraping her nails gently and leaving a wake of gooseflesh. She cupped his balls and squeezed, then plunged his dick deep into her throat.

"Fuck!" Trent cried out. "Adalia, how are you –"

She silenced him with a steady rhythm, using one hand to stroke his shaft and her own saliva as lubricant.

He trembled, grasping at her shoulders, digging his fingers into her flesh. His breath quickened and he groaned, the ache to release was in the tension of his muscles, the rise and fall of his chest.

Adalia stopped sucking and rose. She tipped him back onto the bed and he flopped down, blinking rapidly. Did he really think she couldn't handle this? That she couldn't be the one in control?

She slipped up his body and pressed her breasts into his chest, nipples hardening, rubbing against his pecs.

He grabbed two handfuls of her ass and squeezed hard, then craned his neck to kiss her.

Adalia pushed him back by the forehead with her index finger. She straddled him, reached between her legs and grabbed his dick, then forced it deep into her sex.

"I'm too close," he gasped, still grabbing her ass.

Adalia rode him, moving her body so that he slid in and out of her quivering pussy. "Good," she replied, "I want you to come for me."

"Adalia," he warned.

"I want you to squirt deep inside me. Fill me up with your cum." She flashed him a naughty smile and went harder, and faster, leaning over to brace herself on the sheets and working her ass up and down. Her breasts brushed his face and he opened his mouth, taking one nipple and then the other, burying his head between them.

His cock grew massive inside her. He jammed through his orgasm, and the sensation of him pulsing against her walls sent her over the edge too.

Adalia clenched around him, milking the last of his seed, forcing it deep into her pussy.

Then she rolled off him with a sweet smile and lay on the bed, breathing heavily.

***

Trent settled back in the leather office chair in his study and stared at the papers strewn across the desk. He grasped the tumbler of whiskey and clinked the ice in the glass with a sigh. He'd never been as stressed in his memory. Taking the company's IPO live was a nightmare of paperwork and portfolios, meetings with lawyers and accountants and…

"Don't worry, Mr. Dawson, we can do this."

And Michelle Van Heerden, of course.

She sat across from him, preening her hair with her long fingernails and simpering every time he so much as glanced in her direction. He refused to work from home because being in Michelle's presence drove his wife over the edge and he simply couldn't risk any harm to her health, mental or otherwise.

"We need to host another meeting with the board at the bank," he said, shuffling a few papers together. "There's too much to do here and I don't see how they'll get the private investors in time."

"What about Mr. Harrington? We've already got one private investor."

"Yes, he's one. Only one," Trent replied, raising a finger. "I don't understand it, but the guys at the bank seem to be dragging their feet with this. I need to stir them up a little. There isn't much time left."

Michelle rose from her seat and brushed off her skin tight skirt. She flicked her hair over one shoulder and pressed her breasts out. "Can I get you anything, Mr. Dawson?"

She was shameless. And if it wasn't for a favor he owed to her father, he would've given her the boot a long time ago. Mr. Van Heerden had been an outstanding man, he'd helped Trent follow his dreams in the beginning, given him a kick in the right direction, and now he was burdened with his daughter as his assistant.

It put too much pressure on his relationship with Adalia.

"Yes," Trent replied.

"What is it?" Michelle asked, cracking a smile which would've made Adalia claw her eyes out. Man, he loved how passionate his wife got, and how protective she was over him.

"I need you to contact the bank and organize a meeting. I'm pretty sure I just said that," he said, then gestured to the notepad and pen on the corner of his desk. "Why aren't you writing any of this down?"

Michelle jumped and hurried to the desk. She took a seat, then grimaced and picked up the pen.

"Tell them I want a meeting on Tuesday first thing, and if they can't manage that, we'll be turning to another investment bank to handle our IPO." Trent sipped from the tumbler and checked his watch. It was past 10 at night, but he'd committed himself to doing this right. What future would his kid have if he couldn't handle business?

"At what time?"

"At their earliest convenience. And by that I mean before noon. I won't wait around for this. Be snappy on the phone." Trent chewed his bottom lip and took another sip of the whiskey.

"Should I call them now?"

"What's the time, Michelle?" Trent asked, keeping a straight face. Inside, his blood had started boiling. He didn't want to sit around listening to her for a second longer. He needed a break from work but he couldn't take it. That frustration had built past breaking point.

Van Heerden checked her watch then gave an exaggerated shrug which made her breasts jiggle. "I guess I'll have to handle that tomorrow."

"I guess," he said.

"Is there anything else I can do for you, Mr. Dawson? Anything at all?" Michelle leaned forward, exposing some cleavage. Nothing in comparison to Adalia's.

He averted his eyes and slammed the tumbler down. "No, thank you, that will be all."

"I could stay and –"

"That will be all," Trent repeated, hardening his tone.

Michelle shrugged again, then rose from her chair and bobbed her head. "Goodnight, Mr. Dawson. I'll see you tomorrow again."

"Yeah," he replied then waved her away. The businessman in him was rife with guilt for treating an employee with disrespect, but the husband was filled with determination to rid himself of her.

Michelle turned on her heel and strode out of his office, wiggling her butt.

He lowered his gaze to the papers on his desk, then shuffled them into a semblance of order and separated them into their various files and dossiers. Trent shut his eyes for a moment in between movements, breathing in the scent of his leather chair.

This was only the beginning. In the months to come, there would be hard work to do and then a baby to look after, not to mention trying to keep Adalia in check so she didn't do anything stressful.

His phone buzzed to life on his desk. He frowned and snatched it off the cradle.

"Hello?"

"Oh, so you'll answer the office phone, but not your cell?" Adalia's voice was shrill on the other end.

"Honey, my cell is on silent. I was working." Trent grimaced – this had to be the start of the fabled pregnancy hormones. Well, he was no one's punching bag. "You know I don't like to be bothered when I'm working."

"Not even when it's the anniversary of the day we met?" Adalia snapped out the question.

His heart did a 360 degree turn in his chest. He'd completely forgotten in the stress of work and worrying about what he had to do next. Adalia had mentioned it at least twenty times in the past week.

"I'm sorry. I got caught up at work. Things are stressful lately."

"The dinner's ruined," she replied then she hung up.

The dial tone had never seemed as ominous. He wasn't one to jump at threats, but when Adalia was pissed at him, or even a little bit unhappy, it felt like his entire world would fall apart. Not to mention how the stress could affect the baby.

Trent stood and put the receiver back on the cradle. He left the mess on his desk and strode out of the door.

Chapter Six

Trent got out of the car and waited for the gates at the end of the driveway to close. Not because he thought someone would slip in, but simply because he wanted to delay the inevitable. Adalia was in the house, waiting for him, and she wasn't getting any happier.

He straightened his tie and walked up his front stairs, then pushed the front door open to the foyer. The scent of cooking wafted from the kitchen – it smelled like his favorite: hamburgers and fries.

He dropped his briefcase on the table and straightened his shoulders. She was his wife, not someone he had to be afraid of. The only thing he feared was disappointing her and he'd done that successfully already.

"Adalia?" Their foyer was minimally decorated, though there was a vase of flowers on the walnut table at the end of the vast room. That was her addition, a touch of femininity here and there, mingled with the flavor of her cooking and her perfume on the air.

Trent walked through the hall, footsteps echoing on the marble and made for the doorway on the far end, which led directly into his kitchen. He'd never used it before they'd gotten married. In fact, he'd mostly eaten out or gotten take out, except for the few nights his house-keeper, Macy, would stay late to cook a meal when he got home from work.

His life had been empty without her.

He stepped into the kitchen and stopped in front of the granite topped island in its center.

Adalia stood beside the stove, stirring a pot of mushroom sauce with her back to him. She didn't give any indication that he'd walked in. "Where were you?" she asked, then tapped the end of the spoon on the rim of the pot and placed it on the counter.

"I got caught up at work," he replied. "I'm sorry I missed this. It smells amazing."

"I had to make the mushroom sauce twice." Adalia turned to him, her eyebrows drawn into sharp ticks. She wore a form-fitting red dress which hugged her curves, and a pair of pearl earrings he'd bought for her a few days prior.

"Why?"

"Because the first one spoiled since you didn't make it home on time for our anniversary dinner." She flashed him a sweet smile. That was her 'you're in shit and you're not gonna like it' smile.

"I'm sorry, honey. I've just been hard at work. What with the IPO coming up and –"

"Were you with Michelle?" Adalia slammed the pot of mushroom sauce off the heat and strode up to him. "Answer me."

"Give me a chance!" he snapped. "You're putting pressure on me and yourself right now. You need to calm down, Adalia."

"Was she there?"

"She's my assistant. Of course she was there," he replied. He would never lie to her and he wouldn't evade the truth either.

"So, you chose to spend our anniversary with that blonde bitch instead of with me, your pregnant wife." Adalia glared at him then poked him once in the chest. "I suppose I should've expected as much. Who wants to be with a fat pregnant woman when they can get into –"

"Stop it." Trent grasped her by the wrist and lowered her hand for her. "Stop talking shit. You know I love you and only you, so why are you pushing this?"

"It's our anniversary and you were with her! You know how much I hate her," Adalia growled, then snapped her mouth shut. She probably hated admitting how much she despised Michelle, even though it was pretty clear to him.

"I was at work late for us, for our baby," he said, then paused. A red haze descended and he gritted his teeth. He worked himself to the bone for this shit? To come home and be berated for not being here, when all he wanted to do was look after his family. "It's not a real anniversary anyway."

Adalia froze and glared at him. "Not a real anniversary?"

"Yes, it's not like we've been married for a year." He shook his head and laughed. "You don't even care how hard I've worked for us. You want what you want and if I don't march in step with that then I'm public enemy number one."

"Have you been drinking?" Adalia whispered, folding her arms across her breasts.

"Fuck it. Yes, I've been drinking. I've had a couple of whiskeys because, God dammit, I deserve them after the shit I've been through this week."

"Drinking with Michelle," she murmured, more to herself than to him apparently. "While I'm here slaving away over the stove to make a delicious meal for our –"

"Don't you dare say anniversary," Trent growled. "I have enough stress at work without you adding to it. And God knows, Adalia, we can't afford to have a fight. We don't want to harm the baby."

"Oh, so you think it would be better to let this fight fester?" She walked to the fridge and brought out a soda, then popped the tab and tossed some of it back. "For our unborn child, I mean. Because who the hell cares what I want?"

"What?" Trent shook his head and glanced at the cold cheeseburgers on the countertop. His stomach rumbled.

"That's right. I've become nothing but a carrier. The minute we found out I was pregnant, I became the body holding the baby, rather than your loving wife."

"I've had enough for one night. Sorry, or what the fuck ever you want me to say for this screw up of an evening," he said. He then undid his tie, turned around and walked out of the kitchen. He slammed his feet onto the marble all the way up to their bedroom.

Trent stripped off his shirt and pants and threw them on the dresser, then got into bed and closed his eyes.

***

Adalia stood in the office at the bakery and looked at the potted plant in the corner. It brought back memories of Trent, of Michelle, things that made her stomach turn and then put it at ease seconds later.

She turned and walked back to the chair, then sat down. She was nowhere near showing her pregnancy, but she couldn't help lowering herself carefully, avoiding a bump on the front from the desk. Trent's insistence on caution was infectious.

Adalia clenched her fists and glared at the papers on the desk. Order sheets and other mundane tasks, when really, she wanted to work on her catering business. She hadn't even decided on a name yet.

A knock rattled the door.

That had better not be Trent. "Who is it?" Adalia called out.

The doorknob turned and DeShawn entered, without his do-rag and looking sheepish. "Can I talk to you?"

Adalia's eyes widened and she leaned forward in her seat. Why the hell was he here? "That's not a good idea," she replied. "Honestly, the last time I saw you, you tried to crash my wedding and break Trent and I up. Why the hell would I want to talk to you, of all people?"

"'Cos I love you, baby," he replied, then sauntered a step into the room. He stopped at a single glance from her – it was the iciest one she had in her repertoire.

"You don't know what love is, DeShawn, you never did." She placed a hand across her stomach and held it there, as a form of protection of sorts. Trust was a concept she'd lost long ago, when it came to this man.

Cheating, lying, getting way too physical, and then trying to destroy her wedding day. Yeah, DeShawn could fuck off.

"Yeah, maybe I don't, girl, but you," he said, and stepped towards the desk again, raising one finger, "you's something special. I been watching you, makin' sure you all good. You all safe. I ain't never gonna let you go again."

"I don't have time for this," Adalia replied, then ran her hand across her forehead and wiped away a thin sheen of sweat. She grabbed the remote for the air conditioning unit above the door, and clicked a button. Cool air swept over her skin, thank God for that.

The pregnancy had her running hot. The doctor, an American one this time, said that was totally normal. Everyone reacted in a different way to having a human being growing inside them.

"Hear me out, girl, please. I was at the Trap house thinkin' 'bout you all day." DeShawn shuffled to the chair in front of the desk, shoulders hunching over further with every step he took. "C'mon." He grasped the back of the chair and looked at her expectantly.

"Sit down and talk," she waved then gathered the papers on her desk into a rough pile and patted the end of them.

DeShawn sank into the chair and squished around for a while. He readjusted his too-low jeans and snapped the waistband of his boxers. "So where your man at?" he asked, glancing at the filing cabinet in the corner, like Trent would pop out of it at any second and yell 'surprise, mother fucker!'

"He's working on the IPO for his company," she said, though there wasn't any way he could use that information. *Hopefully*. She still couldn't forgive the cake incident that had basically ruined her.

"Say what?" DeShawn placed his hands on his thighs and tilted his head to one side.

"It's an Initial Public Offering for investors who are interested in the company." Once again, absolutely no point in telling him this. He either wouldn't understand it or would have no interest in it.

"Right, right," he said, bobbing his chin back and forth in a weird head bobble of acceptance. "So that's good. Aight, look," DeShawn said, raising a hand and knocking on the table, "look, I gotta tell you something."

"Oh good God, what is it?" Adalia asked, and managed not to roll her eyes. It was a real challenge though. She tipped her head back and bathed her neck in the gusts of cold from the air conditioner. She took the moment of silence to collect herself, the cool center she'd had once upon a time, before the pregnancy hormones had set in then looked at her ex-boyfriend again. "What do you want to say?"

"I did you wrong, Dalie, I did you real wrong," DeShawn said, then dry-washed his hands. "I gotta say sorry for the whole wedding thing. That was not how shit was supposed to go down."

"Then how was shit supposed to go down?" she asked, tapping her foot beneath the desk, ramming the low heel of her pump into the carpet. "Enlighten me." How could he have envisioned another conclusion to crashing her wedding? For God's sake, he'd told Trent, all the guests, the reverend, that she'd slept with him the night before the wedding.

"I, fuck it, Dalie, I dunno. I was just mad fo' your love," DeShawn grunted then cleared his throat. "So yeah. I'm sorry. Aight?"

"Alright. I'm not going to say I forgive you yet, but thanks for offering an apology. As for the whole 'mad with love' thing. I can't help you with that. I'm married," she said.

"Yeah, I know –"

"And pregnant," she continued, a smile stretching her lips.

Shock clanged into place on DeShawn's face. His jaw dropped, eyes widened and he drew in a massive breath. "No shit."

"No shit. We just found out a short while ago." Adalia rubbed her stomach then glanced at the door. "So, thanks a lot for your apology, but I have to get back to work."

"Sure, sure." DeShawn bobbled his head again then launched himself out of the chair like it was a hot plate. "I'll see ya 'round, Dalie." Then he turned and hurried to the door, without the usual hop in his gait.

Somehow, she doubted she'd ever see that man again. The word 'pregnant' had worked magic. "Don't come back here, DeShawn, never again. Don't call, write, fucking text. Just leave me alone."

DeShawn nodded once, then opened the door and sauntered out of her life.

Chapter Seven

Trent sat at this desk in the study and sipped his espresso. He wasn't that into it this afternoon. He'd have preferred a bourbon, maybe some fine wine, but he felt fucking miserable after last night's booze and the fight with Adalia.

She'd given him the cold shoulder that morning and slipped out the door before they could talk about it. Something about checking on the bakery. Like that was a real excuse. He got the feeling that she'd started hating it there, though he'd only started the damn business to make her happy. To get closer to her actually.

The front door slammed and her footsteps echoed across the marble hall.

He gripped the desk, waiting for her to enter, but she didn't. Instead, those footsteps traversed the stairs and faded. The slam of their bedroom door made him jump in his seat. Yeah, she was definitely still pissed. Better to let that rest a while before he tried broaching the topic. They just didn't understand each other lately.

Adalia was on some weird freedom trip and he was focused on work. Maybe it was a crisis caused by her hormones or some shit.

Trent sighed and dragged his laptop towards himself, staring at the numbers in the columns of the spreadsheet. He blinked and rubbed his eyes. It'd been a long day. He yawned and shoved the half-empty coffee cup to one side.

He was pretty much done. Just one last run through his emails and he'd go upstairs and make up with his wife. Trent smiled at that thought. His wife. He loved calling her that.

He opened up his email client and waited for the inbox to fill up, then scrolled through the messages. Junk mail here, a few emails from clients and… what the fuck? An email from DeShawn Tibbet. That had to be the same DeShawn as…

He squinted at the screen, gaze flicking over the subject line. It read: **THOUGHT YOU SHOULD KNOW**.

All in CAPS. That was typical of the ingrate. He wiggled his head in consideration then opened the message.

What up, man. Just thought you should know that the bun in Dalie's oven is mine. That's right asshole. I'm the baby daddy.

DeShawn

Trent ground his top teeth against the bottom. "This better not be fucking true." He shoved up from the desk, and his cup crashed over, splintering and spreading cold coffee on the calendar.

Trent marched for the door and wrenched it open. "Adalia!" he yelled up the stairs then charged up, two at a time. He stomped down the hallway, insides burning with a rage he'd never experienced before. Not even when that scumbag had appeared at their wedding. "Adalia!" Trent roared.

"What?!" his wife yelled back at him, further spurring on the anger.

He forced the bedroom door open and found her standing there, in nothing but her bra and panties.

"We need to talk," he said, breathing like a winded ox. "Now."

"What is it?" Adalia asked, and reached for her robe hanging from the back of the door.

Trent snatched it down and tossed it at her. "I just got an interesting email. No, it wasn't fucking interesting. It was sickening."

Adalia caught the robe in one hand, and she glared at him as if he'd thrown a shovel at her. She pulled it on and let the front hang open, exposing her juicy breasts. "What was it, Trent?"

"DeShawn emailed me. He told me that the baby, our baby, is actually his baby with you. Yours together. Which means…"

"Which means you're an asshole," Adalia finished for him.

"What?" Trent loosened his tie, then thought better of it and ripped it right the fuck off. "I can't believe that he'd email me about this."

"Yeah, he's not the father of this child, because I never slept with him. Not since we broke up, fucking years ago." Adalia tied the robe now, whipping the ends of the small band of fabric around until she had them in a bow. "I can't believe you'd think this was for real. I told him not to contact me again. I guess he took that as he could contact you instead."

"What do you mean, you told him not to contact you? When did you see him?" Trent demanded. She'd better stay the hell away from DeShawn Tibbet. That baby in her belly, *if* it was his, couldn't be anywhere near that fucking psychopath.

"I saw him today," she replied.

His abs clenched along with his jaw. "Why?"

"He came to see me at the office to apologize for what he did at our wedding. I told him about the pregnancy to get him to leave me alone, but apparently he thought that was a good enough reason to try to ruin our marriage." Adalia spread her hands then stared at him for a moment. "Trent, if you really believe that I cheated on you, I'm happy to do a paternity test."

Except she didn't sound happy. She was downright furious, nostrils flaring, hands on her hips now.

Trent counted to ten, calming his thoughts and the swirl of testosterone coursing through his veins. Man, he'd take that DeShawn loser and pulverize his face into dust. "I don't believe it's the truth," he said finally, after his breath had stopped hitching in his chest, "and I don't want a paternity test, Adalia."

"Well, what a relief," she replied, then turned her back on him and walked to the dresser. She opened the top draw and took out a mirror and a selection of creams, cotton balls and other womanly things he couldn't identify.

"Adalia, I just needed you to know," he said, tucking his hands behind his back and holding them there. "You understand don't you?"

"Get out," she replied.

"What did you say?" Trent growled, walking over to the dresser and placing his palms on it. He studied the side of his wife's face, the tautness of her cheeks. She was angry alright. He should've cooled down before he'd run upstairs to talk to her about this.

But who the fuck could blame him? The thought of another man's child in his wife was beyond painful. He wouldn't be able to handle that. It would ruin their marriage before it'd even started, so yeah, he'd overreacted.

"I said, get out. I have no interest in talking to you for the rest of the evening. Make that the rest of the week," she said, then slammed the lid off one of her pots of cream. She scooped out a finger-sized amount and dabbed it on her chin.

"I'm not going anywhere. How do you think it made me feel? Getting an email like that." Trent grabbed the cream and shoved the lid back on.

"How do you think it makes me feel when you accuse me of fucking my ex-boyfriend and being pregnant with his child, instead of yours?" Her voice rose to a shriek and she turned on him. She slapped the cream off her chin then poked him in the chest. "What the hell were you thinking?"

"That I can't live without you!" Trent yelled back at her.

Adalia blinked a couple times then shook her head. "What do you mean?"

"I mean, I cannot stand the thought of you not being mine. Of your hands near him and not on me. Of that baby not being ours. I love our life together." He rattled the words out, gripping the dresser with one hand and dropping the other to his side. "So yeah, I blew up. I overreacted. Can you fucking blame me?"

Adalia stared at him and time ticked away, the quiet between them hurt his ears. He wanted her to speak to him, even if it was to shout.

She broke the silence with a soft sob, then charged at his chest and wrapped her arms around him.

Trent started and froze, then folded around her too. "Do you have any idea how much I need you in my life?" he murmured into her hair, then pulled back and kissed her forehead. "Do you?"

"It's the same for me," she replied, then craned her neck and brushed her lips against his.

Heat flooded his body immediately and all his blood rushed to his dick. Just one touch and he was hard for her. Their attraction went past her gorgeous, full body, and to the connection within.

"I need you," she whimpered, and kissed him again. "I need you inside me."

"Oh God," he groaned, because that request was too much to resist.

Trent grabbed her by the waist and walked her to the bed, then lowered her onto it, gently. He stripped the robe open and exposed her bra and panties, both of them lacy red. She was so beautiful. So fucking perfectly flawless.

He ripped her thong down and got between her legs, staring at her delicious folds. She was already swollen for him, dripping wet just from a kiss, and his embrace.

Trent ran his finger from her clit down to her entrance and lubricated it, then used it to massage that button of pleasure.

Adalia jerked her hips towards him. "Don't play with me," she whispered, "get that fat cock inside me. Now."

"No," he replied. Then lowered his face to her pussy and buried himself in it. He sucked her clit, slurping and moaning because she tasted so fucking good. He wouldn't ever want to stop this, except his dick throbbed against the inside of his pants.

Trent stuck his tongue inside her, probing her pussy for more of those sweet juices.

Adalia gave a low shriek of pleasure. "Oh my God." She grabbed the top of his head and forced it closer to her.

Fuck, he loved it when she got like this. He slurped up her juices and probed her entrance again, then rose slowly.

"Don't stop," Adalia pleaded, "please don't stop, baby, I need you."

"Who's stopping?" Trent asked, then whipped off his belt and tossed it into the corner. He undid his pants and pulled his dick out, which dripped with pre-cum, then let her admire it for a minute.

"That's all mine," she said, eyes flashing her possession.

"That's right, it's all yours." Trent lowered himself over her, still in his pants, with his cock peering out of them, because he couldn't stand it anymore. He plunged into her, opening her wide.

Adalia clamped her legs around his waist and stared up at him, never breaking eye contact. "Fill me up with your cum, baby."

"You'll make me come like that." Trent pumped inside her, embraced by her warm folds and growing thicker by the second. He loved her special brand of dirty talk.

Trent angled his body and slowed down, so that the base of his dick rubbed against her clit. She was so wet, it was all over his thighs, all over hers. Fuck, he was so close he could barely hold back a second longer.

Adalia moaned and gripped his shoulders, digging her fingernails into his flesh. Her pussy clenched around his dick, massaging it in warmth and wetness. She yowled through her orgasm, tilting her body so he could get deeper.

That desperation for him drove him past the brink. He crashed into his own climax and squirted his seed deep inside her, pulsing so many times that he didn't think it would ever end.

Trent collapsed to the side of his wife, and she snuggled up to him immediately, nuzzling her head against his neck, her arm creeping across his chest.

"I love you," she murmured, then squeezed him tighter for a second. "I'm sorry."

"I'm sorry too," he whispered, then kissed her forehead.

They drifted off to sleep in each other's arms.

Chapter Eight

Adalia sat in the living room with a file open on her lap and her cell on the coffee table. Time had flown, the last three months and in it, she'd focussed on the catering business and getting herself fed. She was ravenous with the baby, but the nausea had gotten worse too.

Trent was so busy with work, he hardly noticed she'd taken it upon herself to do her own business thing. Besides, the bakery ran just fine on its own. Actually, it was turning a huge profit for a small place, and she planned on using every penny of her share in her new endeavour.

The door opened and she jumped, shutting the file on her lap swiftly.

But it wasn't Trent waiting to reprimand her.

"Oh, it's you," Michelle Van Heerden said, prancing into the room in her high heels and right skirt. "I'd hoped to find Trent in here."

"He's at the office," Adalia replied. "You'd know that if you weren't floating around my home all day, looking for a way to get into his pants."

"I like it better when he's in jeans." Michelle strode towards the couch, wiggling her hips. The high heels accentuated her calves and her skinny toned stomach was clear beneath the tight white blouse she'd paired with her skirt. "You have him now. That's it."

"What?" Adalia crossed her legs and placed her hand over her womb, then winced. She felt weird in there this morning, kind of like things were upside down. It didn't make sense, but that was the best way to describe it.

"Do you really think Trent will stay with you? After the baby when you're a mess, that kid and all its crying is going to send him straight into my arms." Michelle opened them wide and stretched her blood red lips into a victorious smile. "Your marriage is the best thing that's ever happened to our relationship."

"You're delusional. You don't have a relationship with Trent." Adalia placed her hands in her lap, covering the file.

Michelle narrowed her eyes. "What's this?" She snatched the file from Adalia's grasp and flipped it open. "Well, well, planning our own business are we? I bet Trent wouldn't be too happy about that. Keeping the baby safe is all he talks about. God, so fucking annoying." She rolled her eyes and flipped through the pages Adalia had printed out, the numbers, the plan.

The air in the room thickened with tension. Adalia stared up at Trent's assistant through a haze of anger. How dare she touch her plans and threaten her on top of that?

Adalia bolted up right and smacked the file out of the bitch's hand, fury searing through her chest and down into her belly. She gripped at it and winced. No, wait, that wasn't the anger. That was something else.

Pain in her womb. Adalia's eyes widened and she stumbled backwards, feeling for the sofa behind her and hunching over.

"What's the matter? The little brat kicking you too hard?" Michelle asked then eyed the papers on the floor with distaste. "You know your little business will never work. I've been working with Trent for some time, and I know a plan that's doomed to fail when I see one." She smirked. "That includes your marriage."

Adalia's ass met the sofa cushions and she leaned back, taking deep breaths, sweat dripping down the back of her neck, onto her spine and pooling at the base of it. The pain receded slightly, but she couldn't concentrate on anything else but her belly.

What the hell had happened? Was the baby okay?

"What? Nothing to say?" Michelle chuckled. "Figures. You're a big mouth when you're around your husband," she paused and shuddered at the word, then continued, "but when you're all alone, trapped in a corner you're just a… uh, a loser. You're weak."

Adalia ignored her and pressed her hands to her stomach again. Sharp pain, then nothing. Please, God let it not be anything serious. Slowly but surely, the pangs receded and the rush of blood in her ears dulled from a roar to a whisper.

She looked up at Michelle. "Get out of here."

"Ah, you can't take it. Alright, that's fine," Michelle said. She nudged the papers on the floor with the toe of her shoe. "Pathetic."

Adalia's anger returned and she stood again, planting fists on her hips. "I said get out of here. I have important things to attend to. No time for the likes of you." The insults didn't have real sting because her heart wasn't in them. Her belly bubbled with anxiety and she placed a hand to her womb every other second, sweeping her palm across it to soothe the baby, then bringing it back to her hip.

"Whatever, I have to get back to Trent anyway. He needs me, as he always has and always will," Michelle said, smacking her lips after the final word.

Agony pierced Adalia's middle section and she doubled over, gripping at herself. "Oh God," she moaned.

"If this is some method to get sympathy –"

"I need to go to the hospital," Adalia whimpered.

"You're fucking with me, aren't you? What a cheap trick. Like, get over yourself." Michelle shifted her feet and didn't move to help her.

Adalia drew in ragged gasps, shuddering against the waves of pain in her abdomen. "Give me my phone."

Michelle waited a second before stepping forward to grab the phone off the table. She shoved it into

Adalia's hand, their fingers brushed then Michelle turned and walked out of the room. She left the door open behind her.

Adalia clutched the cell and dialed the ambulance, one digit at a time, her fingers trembling, mouth dry. The baby had to be okay. It had to be.

***

Adalia sat in the doctor's office, staring at the horrid painting of a dog on the wall. This wasn't the same as the time she'd found out she was pregnant. For one, she'd been through several tests this time, instead of one, and for another, she was totally alone.

Trent was at work with Michelle.

It was afternoon already and she still hadn't called him to tell him something was wrong, because, quite frankly, she didn't need the added pressure of his anxiety. Obviously, Michelle would take this opportunity to get in some extra time with her husband, the bitch.

Adalia clutched the straps of her handbag on her lap, then released slowly. She had to relax, but this had been a stressful day.

Her pains had stopped before the ambulance had arrived and she'd actually managed to walk to the van and tell them what was wrong. They'd taken her to the hospital right away, because pregnancy was dangerous, apparently.

71

Adalia clicked her teeth and waited. The doctor would be in soon, according to the surly nurse with a clipboard, to tell her what the problem was. Or what the problem had been. She ran her palm over her stomach again, licking her lips.

The office door opened and she turned slightly. An old white guy in an even whiter doctor's coat entered, carrying a file folder. He smiled warmly at her.

"Adalia, how are you holding up?" Dr. Matheson asked, shutting the door behind himself to afford them privacy. He walked around the massive walnut desk and took a seat in leatherback chair. He swivelled from side to side for a moment, then placed the folder on the desk and leaned on it with both hands. "No pains since we last spoke?"

"Nothing," she replied, gripping her womb then stroking it again. She'd never felt so protective over a human in her life, not even Trent. She couldn't let anything happen to this child, but she had to be the perfect mother for it, and that meant being more than a housewife.

"That's good news," Matheson replied, nodding so that the loose flesh underneath his chin wobbled. He flipped open the file and picked up a few pieces of paper. "The baby, you'll be glad to know, is fine."

"Oh thank God." Adalia wilted with a relief, bottom lip quivering in an effort to keep back the tears. "Thank God."

"But there's something else that's come to my attention that I think you –"

The office door banged open behind them. "Adalia!" Trent stood there, eyes wide and fingers gripping the doorjamb. "Adalia, what happened? Michelle said –" He broke off and met the doctor's gaze. "What's going on?"

"I'm sorry, doctor, I tried to stop him," a receptionist said, from behind Adalia's husband. The woman gripped a clipboard to her chest and chewed on the end of a green pen.

"That's quite alright, Betty," the doctor replied, then reshuffled the notes. "Mr. Dawson?" Dr. Matheson asked, looking at Adalia for her nod then stretching his lips into an uncomfortable smile when he got it. "Please take a seat."

The receptionist backed away slowly, wincing at her failure. Trent strode into the room and shut the door carefully, then took a seat beside his wife. "Can someone tell me what the hell is going on?"

"The baby is fine, Mr. Dawson, I was just telling Adalia here about her test results." Matheson shifted in his leather chair.

Adalia refused to meet her husband's gaze, didn't reach for his hand either. She stared at the doctor, pulse thrumming against the skin of her neck. "What is it? What did the tests say?"

"Your blood test, the Progesterone Test particularly, revealed that you have low progesterone levels," Matheson said, then cleared his throat. He took a sip of water from a glass on the corner of his desk.

"What does that mean?" Trent demanded, sitting straight as an arrow.

"Adalia's about three months along now, which is usually when the placenta takes over progesterone production. This is a dangerous time for the fetus, because too little progesterone means a higher risk of spontaneous abortion."

"That's a lot of scary words in one sentence," Adalia observed, blinking rapidly to keep tears at bay. She was an emotional wreck lately.

"Get to the point," Trent growled.

"Stop it," Adalia whispered to him.

"That's quite alright." Matheson waved at her then continued. "The abdominal pain you experienced was because of low progesterone levels. It's a dangerous condition, but it's treatable." He scratched the tip of his bulbous nose and sniffed. "I don't want you to be alarmed by this. It's imperative that you stay calm and rested."

Adalia bit her bottom lip hard. She was terrified. Trent slipped his hand into her lap and she squeezed it tight, leeching off any comfort she could get from him. "What's the treatment?" she asked, choking out the question.

"We'll give you one immediate progesterone injection, and after that a supplement course." The doctor took out a prescription pad from his desk drawer and started scribbling things down. "I'm going to give this to a nurse and she'll get it sorted out for you, alright?" He studied their expressions then frowned. "This is a potentially fatal condition for the baby, but if you follow your medication and take it easy, both of you will be fine. Alright?"

"Yes," Adalia breathed, but she couldn't hold the tears back a second longer. They dripped from her eyelids and ran down her cheeks.

"I'll give you two a moment, get this to the nurse," Matheson said, giving them both a sympathetic look, before rising from his chair and leaving the room. The door clicked closed behind him and Adalia slumped forward, resting her forearms on the desk. Sobs racked her body, but there was no pain, at least.

"Easy, it's going to be alright, my love, we'll make it through this," Trent murmured, stroking the back of her neck.

Adalia bit her bottom lip. He was wrong. Nothing would ever be alright again.

Chapter Nine

Adalia walked through the front door, with arms folded and misery written all over her face. She wiped her cheeks and stopped in the hall, staring up at the second floor and chewing the inside of her cheek.

Their home looked different now. She couldn't place what it was, but the joy she'd had at being here with Trent had seeped out of her. She was exhausted.

"It's going to be okay, love. Let's get you upstairs so you can sleep," Trent slung his arm around her waist and walked her up the stairs, holding her close.

His warmth made her want to cry all over again. She'd been so mean to him, they'd fought on and off these past few months because he was so damn busy with work and she wanted more of his time, away from Michelle.

Adalia blinked and looked at him askance. "How did you find out I was at the doctor's?"

"I came home with Michelle to work late and couldn't find you. She told me what happened," he replied, through gritted teeth.

The bitch had waited until the last minute. That was better for Adalia. Trent's outbursts in the doctor's office had done nothing good for her jangling nerves. She was raw with anxiety, ready to collapse from the weight of depression.

What would this mean for her baby? What if the worst became a reality and she lost the little one? Adalia gripped Trent tighter. That couldn't happen. She wouldn't let it happen.

They reached the top of the stairs and her husband pulled her closer and kissed her lightly on the top of the forehead. "I won't let anything happen to you or the baby. I swear to you," he whispered, fiercely. He gripped her for a moment longer, breath hot on her forehead, then kissed her one more time and turned back to the hall.

They walked together, his arm around her shoulders, bringing her small comfort, right to the door of the bedroom. He opened it for her and escorted her in, then stopped and frowned at the papers strewn all over the bed. "What's this?" Trent asked, letting go of her and grabbing one of the sheets of paper.

Adalia frowned and shook her head. She had no idea what they were or why they were on their bed. She braced her back against the doorjamb. "Hasn't Maria been in today?"

Their housekeeper would never allow something like this.

"She was, that's what's so weird." Trent glanced at her then studied the first page, his frown turned to a wide-eyed glare, then anger. He picked up the next page on the bed then another and another, reading through them and flipping them back down.

"What is it?"

Trent marched towards her, lifting one of the sheets of paper. "You tell me, Adalia."

She took it from him then, gaze roving over the words typed on the page. It was the plan for her catering business. She'd left the papers down in the living room, anticipated that they'd get cleaned and put away. Instead, they ended up in the bedroom.

"Michelle," she uttered, page shaking in her grip. "She brought this up here."

"Answer my question, Adalia. What is this?" Trent demanded, folding his arms and planting his feet.

She was cornered now. There was no way to deny that she had her own plans. Ones he thought would endanger the baby. They'd never agreed on this point.

"It's a business plan. I told you I wanted to go into catering, Trent." Adalia replied, then pushed off from the door and walked to the bed. She picked the pages off and started reorganizing them.

"These dates are set for pretty fucking soon," he snapped, "before the baby's due date."

"And so?" Adalia asked, turning to grab the last page from him. She organized it into a pile and held it to her chest. "What about it?"

"What about –?" Trent cut off and sputtered wordlessly for a few moments. "We just spoke to the doctor about taking it easy!" He exploded then moderated his tone. "Adalia, you can't dedicate all your energy to this. It's fucking crazy."

"Why?! Why is it so damn crazy that I want to create a better future for myself and our child?" She gripped the papers so hard they crumpled a little. Why couldn't he understand this?

"We won't have a child if you carry on this way," Trent grated. "You on your feet all day long? Do you really think that's wise?"

"It can't hurt to get some exercise and I won't be on my feet all day long." Adalia sat down on the edge of the bed then popped up again. Trent would probably take it as a sign that she needed her rest and use it against her in the argument.

"Just how much exercise have you been getting? Maybe the whole reason the baby is in danger is because you…" Trent didn't finish the sentence.

"Really. That's what you think? That walking around has miraculously cut off my progesterone supply?" Adalia shrieked. "That I'm endangering our child by striving for a better future?!"

Trent growled, stopped then did it again. "You know what? Yes. That's exactly what I fucking think. All you care about is yourself in this situation. Not how this could affect our baby! We spoke about this," he said, gripping handfuls of his hair for the briefest moment, then letting go, "I mean we actually spoke about this. I thought I got through to you, for fuck's sake."

Adalia glared at him, air whistling through her nostrils with each breath. *Got through to her.* He'd thought he got through to her about being ambitious? About having dreams. He really didn't know her at all.

Adalia walked to the bedroom door.

"Where are you going?" Trent asked. "Adalia, answer me."

"To my father's. Don't bother contacting me until you realize that I'm a woman, not an oven." She slammed the bedroom door behind her and marched down the stairs.

It felt like the beginning of the end. Tears flowed down her cheeks afresh.

***

Adalia sat on the front porch of her father's house and leaned against the railing, with the sun on her knees and her business plan in her lap. A week had passed and Trent still hadn't come to see her. She'd asked him not to, so it made sense that he hadn't. He had tried calling though, a lot, and the tone of messages he left her became increasingly angry.

Trent didn't like losing what he wanted.

She chewed the end of the pen and studied her plans. "I can do this," she murmured. Adalia stroked her womb again, which had finally started to show a little. "We can do this, baby."

Missing Trent was a constant heartache. She was furious with him, and she wouldn't cave, but that didn't mean she loved him any less. Adalia squared her shoulders and turned back to her plan, losing herself in the numbers for a moment, the sheer gravity of what she wanted to take on.

She could make herself the catering business to beat in this city, if she did it right. It was all about planning, and if things went really badly with Trent, God forbid, she needed to make money to support this child.

"Dalie, thought I find you here." DeShawn's voice slithered through the morning air and pierced her hearing.

She placed the pen on top of her papers and looked up, intestines twisting with irritation. Of course he'd found her, the fucking psychopath. It wasn't enough that he'd tried to destroy her wedding or claim ownership of her child. Now, he'd tracked her down and decided to hound her on home turf.

"DeShawn," she said, and made her tone gravelly with displeasure. She eyed his Timberlands and the jeans he'd finally decided to wear at a normal height. He'd put on a white wife beater – how damn appropriate. "Have you come to give me another of your fake apologies, because I'm not interested."

"Apologize fo what?" he asked, grabbing at his balls and readjusting them, like she wasn't right there.

Adalia pulled a face and got up, so she wouldn't be on the same level as his scratching hand. "Don't play dumb. Once again, you tried to ruin my relationship."

"I didn't ruin shit." DeShawn leaned to one side and gripped his left arm with his right.

"Oh really? Then the email my husband received was from someone else. You know another DeShawn Tibbet? I'd be interested to meet the man who thinks he can take ownership of my child," she snapped. Adalia walked to the front door to escape him, but DeShawn was notoriously difficult to escape.

The idiot followed her onto the porch, clumping around in those yellow boots like he owned the place.

"Just back off," she said, opening the front door and leaning in to drop the documents on the entrance hall table. She turned back to him and slammed the door shut. "Say what you have to say, real quick, before I lose my patience and kick you off my front porch."

"Don't threaten me, woman," DeShawn replied, raising a finger.

Adalia grabbed it and twisted it back. "Don't raise your finger at a pregnant woman."

He looked like he wanted to hit her, but the scowl died after a few minutes of hard thinking. Or maybe it was plain thinking. DeShawn wasn't the sharpest utensil in the drawer.

"Let go," he growled.

Adalia held on a second longer, narrowing her eyes then released him. "What do you want, DeShawn? What is it this time?"

"Do I gotta want somethin' jus' to come see you?" He did his weird gripping one arm with the other lean again. Kind of like a failed model pose.

"Yes, of course you do. Why did you tell Trent the baby is yours?"

"'Cos," he said, then paused and looked back over his shoulder, then at the window closest to them, which looked in on the tiny dining room of the house. "'Cos we meant to be together, girl. Like, that's my kid, you know?"

"There's no one here. Cut the crap."

"I ain't lying," DeShawn replied, gaze shifting from the end of the porch to her expression and then to the front door behind her.

Either he was delusional or he was desperate to be with her. Why? Why did he want her this badly when he'd practically thrown her away during their relationship?

"Money?" Adalia asked it out loud.

"Huh?" DeShawn scratched his temple with his fingernail and pouted his lips. "I ain't got no money, girl. If I did, you'd be my woman."

"Because I'm a gold digger, apparently. I don't have time for this. I have an unborn child to worry

about and a business to build from the ground up."
Adalia stopped talking for a second and licked her lips.
"How did you know I'd be here?"

"Heard around town," he said, and shrugged, then
caught her hand. "Dalie, I need you back. Need you as
my woman."

She ripped her hand from his grip. He'd keep on
doing shit like this until she got rid of him for good. A
group of guys walked past the house, glancing up at it
and adjusting their low-slung pants, laughing in their
group, messing around. At least somebody was happy.

"Alright, DeShawn, you can have me," she said,
and he lurched forward to embrace her. She put her
hand up and slammed it into his chest. "If you take a
paternity test to prove you're the father of my baby."

DeShawn's expression of triumph faltered. Ha!
There was no way those results would come back
positive for him. She hadn't slept with him since they'd
dated. But if he wanted to play delusional, then she
could too.

Maybe this would prove to Trent that she wasn't a
sleazebag, and get rid of her ex once and for all.

"Do you agree?" Adalia asked, tilting her ear
towards him to listen for his answer.

DeShawn's bottom lip quivered.

Chapter Ten

Adalia crossed her hands in her lap and shifted uncomfortably. The doctor, this one a specialist in paternity testing, sat across the table, looking at the three of them, sitting in a row. Trent on her right side, sitting rod straight in his chair and gripping the armrests. DeShawn on her left, slumped down and fiddling on his cell phone.

"The procedure is relatively simple," said the doctor, a woman with creamy brown skin and her hair tied up in a harsh ponytail. "I will take buccal swabs from either of the men then withdraw a sample from the fetus."

Adalia gulped for air and scrunched the corner of her cotton dress. "A blood sample?"

"It's a good thing you waited until 16 weeks. The initial physical exam showed that your baby is at the right age for amniocentesis."

"I don't like this, Adalia," Trent said immediately, giving the doctor the evil eye. "I don't like the idea of anything touching our child."

"Me neither," DeShawn said.

"You shut the fuck up." Trent leaned forward and raised a finger at the other man in the room. "You're a second away from getting pounded."

"There will be none of that in my office," said Dr. Chowdhury. "This is a place of peace, not one of violence." She straightened a picture on her desk, one of two healthy, happy children and a golden retriever.

Trent sat back with a huff, and DeShawn folded his arms.

"Please tell me more about this uh –" Adalia interrupted, hoping to get the conversation back on track.

"Amniocentesis," Dr. Chowdhury said, then nodded her encouragement. "We insert a needle into your womb and withdraw some of the amniotic fluid for testing. This is the fluid which surrounds the child. We don't physically touch or harm the unborn child in any way."

Adalia shot a look at DeShawn, hating him with every fiber of her soul. If it wasn't for him, she wouldn't be in this goddamn situation. Scratch that, she should never have asked him for the test in the first place, but she'd never thought it would be this scary.

"What are the dangers for the baby?" Trent asked, moving to the edge of his chair.

"Yeah," DeShawn echoed, after a couple seconds had passed.

A vein in Trent's temple throbbed, and he strained his neck forward as if actively trying to avoid making any kind of contact with Adalia's ex.

"There is a 0.5% chance of miscarriage. But this is a very rare situation. Very rare." Dr. Chowdhury stressed the point by raising her palms above her desk and pulsing them up and down. "I assure you that my staff are more than capable of performing the procedure safely."

"No, fuck this," Trent said, and his skin turned ruddy. "No, you can't do that."

"Yeah, ain't gonna do that, no way," DeShawn added in.

Dr. Chowdhury's dark eyebrows bobbled up and down, she shared her confusion with Adalia. "Why did you come?"

"I want this done. But I'm on progesterone supplements because of low progesterone levels. I'm not sure that it's worth the risk," Adalia whispered, though she glanced askance at DeShawn.

He didn't want the paternity test either, and there was one reason for that. He knew he couldn't possibly be the father.

"It's that or wait until the baby is born, then take the blood." Dr. Chowdhury observed. She picked up her pen off the side of the desk and hovered it over a pad. "What is the name and number of your current OBGYN?"

Adalia took out her cell and gave the doctor the details in a drone of defeat. This had been her sure fire method of ridding herself, and Trent, of DeShawn once and for all.

"I'll return in a moment. I'm just going to give your doctor a call and get his thoughts on this procedure," Dr. Chowdhury said. She excused herself from the room, leaving them in a silence which was beyond awkward.

DeShawn shifted in his chair and scratched his balls. Trent sat dead still again, staring straight ahead, but with sweat streaking down his cheeks. That vein in his temple hadn't disappeared either.

Her husband was clearly furious at being here in the first place. "We didn't have to do this," he said, without facing her. "I told you I believed you."

"This is more than that," Adalia whispered back, between her teeth, though DeShawn could definitely hear what they had to say.

"What?" Trent tilted his head slightly and looked at her out of the corner of his eye. "What do you mean?"

"Don't you see? He will never leave me alone, never leave us alone unless we get rid of him for good. Can you think of a better way?" Adalia asked.

DeShawn didn't comment, just picked at his front teeth with a toothpick he drew from his sagging front pocket.

"That's what this is all about? Getting rid of him? You sure?" Trent questioned, facing forward again.

"What exactly are you insinuating?"

"That there's a possibility this test might go the wrong way," Trent replied, clenching his jaw.

Adalia went numb. She'd never considered how this might look to her husband. Her insistence on doing the test had affected him because he thought there was a reason for it. That made her angry. But she understood it. She understood how that looked.

Adalia grabbed his hand swiftly and squeezed once. "That is the only reason, Trent."

He didn't squeeze her hand back, but he didn't push her away either.

The door opened and Dr. Chowdhury entered, wearing a broad smile. She hurried to her desk and sat down. "Yes, I spoke to your doctor. He's on board with this procedure. He said that it would be safe for the baby."

Adalia looked at Trent, then to DeShawn, who was a lot sweatier than usual.

"Good," she said, and curved her lips into a nervous smile. "Let's do this."

***

Adalia lay on the sofa in the living room with her feet up and her eyes closed. The baby was fine, and she didn't have any pain in her abdomen, even after Dr. Chowdhury had withdrawn the sample.

Her father was at work late, the TV was on in the background – some weight loss special, ugh – and she had a mac 'n cheese in the oven. This was as peaceful as it got, given the circumstances.

Adalia let that sense of calm wash over her, twiddling her bare feet. She wanted to believe everything would be okay. She'd stay positive and attack her business ideas in the morning. She'd already found a place to set up the kitchen and had the website ready to go.

"Adalia," Trent spoke above her.

She jumped and gave a tiny shriek, then settled back on the couch. "How did you get in here?" she asked, pulse pounding from the fright.

"The front door was unlocked," he replied, smoothing the long sleeves of his shirt, "which I've got to say is unwise."

Adalia sat up slowly, pushing herself into position with her palms and swinging her legs over the side of the sofa. "What are you doing here, Trent?" She breathed the words out, because inside she was overwhelmed. She wanted him there, but she didn't at the same time.

Adalia pressed her palms together and waited.

Trent didn't say anything. He towered over her, looking down at the top of her head with softness in his gaze and his arms loose at his sides. "I'm sorry," he grunted.

Adalia swallowed and fingered the threads of the sofa's material cover. "For what?"

"Adalia," he groaned, then ran his hand through his hair and messed it up. It stood on end, which was even sexier than when he had it styled. "I'm sorry for doubting your motives at the doctor's yesterday. And for trying to make you give up on what you want to do."

"Thank you," she replied, rising from her seat and facing him. Her guard was still up – surely that couldn't be it? He'd been so set on making her into his perfect little housewife.

"I don't see you as my possession, if that's what you think. Or just the carrier of my child. I'm fucking horrified that my actions came across that way." He glanced at the TV in the background.

Adalia swiped the remote off the arm of the sofa and clicked the *off* button, shutting out the incessant yammering of a health guru with an insanely toned body.

"Thank you," Adalia said, again.

Trent moved in to hold her but she stopped him with her palm up.

"That doesn't mean I'm ready to forgive you, yet. You made me feel guilty." She folded her arms beneath her breasts.

Her husband stared at her for a couple minutes, mouth working around his answer. He turned his back and walked to the door, then came back again. "I didn't mean to make you feel that way. I was just concerned that you would overwork yourself and end up in a tough spot."

"So you thought fighting with me would be the best option?"

Trent threw his arms up in the air. "You don't think I'm stressed about this too? Why do you think I've been spending so much time away from home, working on the IPO? Because I like being away from you?"

She gave him a blank stare in return.

"Michelle. You think it's because I want time with Michelle," Trent replied, then pressed the heels of his palms to his eyes. "You need to let go of that, Adalia. I've told you over and over again that I have no interest in her."

"You don't know what it's like to see you with her. You don't know what she's like when you're not around," she replied. Jealousy reared its deformed head. The kind that made Adalia irrational and actually gave her stomach pains. She massaged her belly.

Trent's irritation morphed into concern. "What's wrong? Is it the baby?" He reached for her and she batted his hand away.

"It's indigestion. Anyway, Michelle doesn't matter. I just… I need you to be at home sometimes and I need you to understand that I will follow through with this catering business." Adalia set her jaw and stared him down.

Trent stared right back, mimicking her facial expression. He was as stubborn as she was. Maybe that was why they were so drawn to each other. Determined and stubborn, with ambition thrown in.

"Adalia," Trent said, breaking the tension first, "I will do my best to be at home more often, if you will do your best to take it easy."

"I can't –"

"Stop," he said, cutting across her protest. "I'm not saying you shouldn't go ahead and follow through with what you want to do, what you're passionate about. I admire your tenacity, my love." His tone softened by increments, until it was the melted chocolate of voices. The kind that made her want to wrap her arms around his neck. "I'm saying take it easy. Don't over exert yourself while you're doing this."

Adalia went quiet, tapping her cheek with a manicured fingernail. "Alright. I'll go slow. I'll do my best."

"Good, I'm happy with that. All I've cared about is keeping you and our child safe. I love you. I want you to be happy," he said, and opened his arms.

She rushed into them at last, and breathed in the scent of his cologne, burying her face in the crook of his neck.

Trent stroked her back, then ran both hands up to her shoulders and massaged gently. "It's time for you to come home."

Chapter Eleven

"They said it would take five to ten days." Trent paced up and down in his study. "It's been eleven. I'm going to phone that doctor in a minute. What was her name?"

"Dr. Chowdhury," Adalia replied, and flicked through another page in her fashion mag. She loved fashion, she loved food, and her mind was at ease. Trent, however, was the picture of anxiety. Seriously, if she'd looked the term up in a dictionary, his picture would've been there.

"How can you be this relaxed?" Trent asked, folding his arms, then plonking down in his office chair. He immediately swiveled from side-to-side, glaring at her over the desk.

"Because I already know the outcome of the test, honey. The baby is yours. Unless immaculate conception has suddenly become an option." Adalia flashed him a smile brimming with confidence.

She felt better than she'd felt in her entire pregnancy. She'd hired help to get the catering business going, a website designer had perfected the webpage, and the unborn baby was healthy.

"Only five more months to go," she murmured and broke out a smile.

"What now?" Trent asked, wiping sweat off his brow and glaring at his office phone as if it'd offended him.

"Nothing, love. You need to stress less about this. It's your baby and you know that. Right?" Adalia asked, closing the magazine and raising both eyebrows.

"Of course I do. It's not about that, Adalia. Don't you see?" Trent smoothed his fingers over the desk calendar until they bumped off the end and hit the wood behind it. "This could scare that stupid shit off for good."

"Who? DeShawn?" Adalia asked, though she already knew the answer. "Man, I hope you're right. I can't stand dealing with him anymore."

"I hope I'm right too. The sooner we get the call, the sooner we can contact him about it," Trent replied.

"I want to do that." Adalia narrowed her eyes, and vengeance bubbled in the back of her mind for a second. She giggled and slapped the fashion magazine on the desk. "I want to hear the sound of his voice when I tell him the results."

"He has to know that the baby isn't his. I don't get why he went through with it."

Adalia shook her head. "I think it was his final attempt at making us uncomfortable. Or separating us." She lowered her gaze. DeShawn had come close with that, not that she'd ever take him back after what'd happened. She had only one love, and that love would last through thick and thin. And fake paternity tests too.

"Fuck him," Trent growled.

The phone trilled to life on his desk and he flinched, then snatched up the receiver and pressed it to his ear. "Hello? Yes, this is Mr. Dawson. Yes, she's right here." He held out the phone to Adalia, and whispered, "It's Dr. Chowdhury."

Adalia took the phone from him. "Doctor?"

"Good afternoon, Mrs. Dawson. How are you today?"

"I'm anxious to hear the results of the test," she said.

"Yes, usually we call all the involved parties into the office to deliver the results, but we can't get hold of Mr. Tibbet," the doctor replied, with a snap to her tone. "I felt a phone call would be easiest."

"Great," Adalia said. A phone call suited her just fine. It wasn't like they'd need counselling after the results or something. "What can you tell me?"

"Your husband is the father of your child," Dr. Chowdhury replied. "We'll continue with trying to get hold of Mr. Tibbet."

Adalia didn't feel a hint of triumph at the news. She'd known it all along. "That won't be necessary,

Doctor. I'll contact him myself." Then she hung up and gazed at her husband. "You're the father, obviously."

"When do we get it on paper, so we can send it straight to that asshole?" Trent asked, pressing his palms together then making fists.

"I forgot to ask. I'll email the doctor and find out later. Right now, I've got a phone call to make."

"Put him on loudspeaker," Trent commanded, leaning back in his leather chair with an expression which would've been better suited to a mob boss in a Godfather movie.

Adalia chuckled and dialed the number. It rang a few times then clicked over to DeShawn's voicemail.

Scratching crackled on the line. "Yo, this DeShawn. Leave a message." The beep followed, but Adalia hung up without leaving anything for her ex.

"What are you doing?" Trent frowned and rose, coming around the desk to her. "Why don't you try him again?"

Adalia let the question hang in the air for a while and looked around her husband's wood and leather decorated office. She'd like to take a shot at refurnishing this room, like she'd wanted to with the rest of the house, but the catering business would have to come first.

She turned her attention back to Trent again. "He never deserved my time, and I have a feeling he already knows, Trent. I don't think he's coming back again.

Besides, we've got much more important things to worry about."

And this time, she felt it in the bottom of her soul. DeShawn was out of their lives for good. They could continue without worrying about his interference at last.

"Still, wish I could have heard his voice when he found out."

"He probably would've denied the test results, love. He's totally delusional." Adalia placed the phone back in its cradle and rose to meet her husband. "Finally, we can focus on just us, the baby, the businesses."

"This is the beginning of the rest of our lives." Trent wrapped his arms around her waist and pulled her into a hug. He planted a mushy kiss on her forehead then laughed. "Our lives with our child."

Adalia was filled with joy. It was almost too good to be true.

***

Adalia stood in front of the fridge, holding her belly. Being seven months pregnant was no joke. Every time she sat down, her ribs hurt, and the baby loved, seriously loved, playing soccer with her bladder.

She looked around at the cool steel work benches and shining equipment and gave herself a pat on the back. In a few months she'd kitted out the entire kitchen and hired staff. It'd taken a lot of hard work, but she was almost there.

Opening of the catering business was planned for after the baby was born, when she was ready to get back to work… which would hopefully be soon. Maternity leave couldn't take that long, could it?

Adalia grabbed a few pots and pans from an open box on the counter and bent to pack them away. Her stomach grumbled and pain spread in her abdomen. A quick sharp jab and then it was gone again. She froze and touched her hand to her womb, then bit her bottom lip.

That was nothing. It couldn't be the baby. Besides, she was still on her progesterone supplements and she hadn't skipped a single day's worth.

The kitchen doors swung open and Trent marched in, wearing his suit and tie. "I thought I'd find you here," he said, and there was a hint of disapproval to it.

Adalia straightened and left the pots on the floor, lidless and disorganized. She steadied herself on the counter and swiped at the sweat on the bridge of her nose. God, it could be snowing outside and she'd still be covered in brine like a pickled piggy.

"I'm almost done, baby. I've pretty much achieved my goal," she replied, opening her arms wide to encompass the kitchen.

Trent dragged a chair from beside the door and parked it in front of her. "Take a rest. You deserve it."

Even though he'd agreed that she needed to work on her dream, on her own stuff, there were hints of his displeasure in their everyday conversations. This was one of them, but she let it slide.

Adalia lowered herself into the chair and gripped the arms for support, then sat back with a sigh. "Yeah, that's good," she whimpered, then shuffled a bit.

"I've just been at work too. God, what a total fuck up."

"Really? Why?" Adalia asked then winced. Her stomach really didn't feel right. Super uncomfortable and she was so tired she could barely think straight, let alone focus on Trent's work drama.

"Just the whole shuttle launch. It's driving me up the wall. Especially the media behind it."

"Shuttle launch?" Adalia frowned and slipped her feet out of her shoes, then stretched her toes. "What shuttle launch?"

"We're doing it as a publicity stunt to commemorate the IPO. It's set to take place on the same day." Trent paused and tilted his head to one side. "Honey, are you okay? You don't look so good."

"Thanks, love. That makes me feel so good. I'm pregnant, that's my only problem." Adalia said, dripping sarcasm. Now that he mentioned it, she didn't feel her best. But it was probably one of many pregnancy related ailments.

"I can't believe we're almost there," she whispered, then stroked her belly. The baby kicked and she beckoned Trent with a smile.

He placed his hands on her belly and bent down low, placing his mouth close to her skin. Adalia lifted her shirt so he could get even closer. "Hi, baby, I'm your daddy. How are you doing in there?" Trent said, stroking her stomach and raising shivers on her skin. "I can't wait to meet you, little one."

"Do you think we should've found out what the sex was?" Adalia had been contemplating going behind his back and bribing the damn doctor to find out, but Trent had insisted they keep it a surprise until the very end. It hadn't left that much room for decorating the nursery.

"No, of course not," he said then shot her a suspicious look. "You'd better not know, Adalia." He laughed and ran his hands along her belly and around to her back, then pulled himself close and gave her stomach a kiss. "You're the most beautiful pregnant woman I've ever seen."

Adalia smiled and the baby kicked again. It was strange… the little one was never this active, especially late at night. Maybe she overdid it with unpacking the kitchen today.

The kicks stopped and were replaced by shooting pains. Cramps which spread through her womb, rippled through her muscles. Adalia doubled over and gripped her womb. "Oh my God," she choked.

"What's wrong?" Trent asked, eyes going as wide as saucers. "Fuck, is it the baby?"

The pain continued, and it was worse than the one she'd had before. This felt like labor. "Shit," she croaked, "call an ambulance, now."

Trent brought out his cell, crouched in front of her and dialed the number. He pressed the phone to his ear, knuckles white, and began speaking, but it was all Adalia could do to focus on breathing. She didn't hear a word of the conversation.

Her insides convulsed. The baby didn't kick again. Terror clawed Adalia's throat to shreds and she sobbed. This wasn't meant to happen. She'd taken the progesterone. She wasn't due yet for another month.

Another contraction wracked her body and her vision went black from the pain. She held herself together, gripping at her abdomen and panting hard. "Ambulance," she whispered. That was the only word she had. "Ambulance," she repeated, breaking up the syllables painfully slow.

Trent's pale face hovered in front of her at the end of a tunnel of blackness. "It's okay," his voice echoed. "Honey, it's okay, they're on the way. Everything's going to be fine, Adalia. Do you hear me? Everything's going to be okay."

He didn't sound convinced.

Adalia wasn't either. She bent over her belly, guarding the child inside her. If anything happened to her baby, nothing would ever be okay again.

Chapter Twelve

She lay staring up at the lights in the ambulance, breathing slowly. She had an oxygen mask on though she was pretty sure she didn't need it. The pain was gone again, and she'd felt the baby kick.

"Mrs. Dawson?" A medic appeared, a calm black woman with her hair tied in a tight bun. "Can you hear me?"

Adalia nodded and tried for a weak smile. She managed a twitch at the corners of her lips.

"Good. That's good. Your baby is fine, Mrs. Dawson. It's no longer in distress. You can relax," she said, then afforded Adalia a quick smile. "We're taking you to the hospital for observation and we've contacted Dr. Matheson on your husband's insistence."

Adalia reached up and snapped off the oxygen mask, wincing at the pain from the tug of an IV tube in her arm. "Thank you. Where is he?"

"The doctor?"

"Trent. My husband," Adalia whispered then rolled her eyes from side-to-side, searching for him. "Where's my husband?"

"I'm here," he said, from her right side. She craned her neck upwards and caught a glimpse of him sitting along the wall of the van, amidst the medical instruments. His face was a cloud. She couldn't read it.

The medic pushed her head back down gently. "You need your rest, Mrs. Dawson. Please don't strain yourself."

"Yeah, good luck with that," Trent murmured, but the medic didn't hear him. Or if she did, she didn't react. The woman got up and disappeared from view. The back doors of the van slammed, and the cool flow of air from outside was cut off.

Sweat popped up on Adalia's forehead immediately. She didn't have the energy to swipe it off, but she left the oxygen mask hanging to one side and shifted her head slowly to look at Trent.

Her husband sat there with his arms folded staring directly ahead. He oozed anger from every pore. He didn't want to be in the van. He didn't want to be anywhere near her, she could just tell.

"The baby is fine," she croaked, trying to get him to look at her. She was miserable, no longer in pain, but totally exhausted, physically and emotionally. She needed him right now. She needed his support. "Did you hear, Trent? The baby is going to be fine."

"We don't know that yet," he replied, through gritted teeth. "We still have to see the doctor and find out if there was any lasting damage."

Her heart skipped a beat and it reflected on the monitor attached to her.

The medic's voice spoke from the left at the back of the van. "Sir, please don't stress her out. She's been through enough already."

"Yeah, and whose fault is that?" Trent shot back at the woman. The glint in his eyes were feral… an anger she'd never seen in him before.

"Sir?" The medic's voice filled with confusion. "We're almost at the hospital. If you could sit back and relax, that'd be great."

"I can't relax. My child is in danger," Trent argued back.

His child was in danger. Not his wife, just his child. He didn't care that she'd been in agony, or that she was afraid. Trent only cared about himself and the baby. When had she left the room? Hell, when had she left their marriage entirely?

"I assure you, the baby is in no imminent danger. Your wife, however, is in a delicate state. I suggest you quiet down," the medic's tone hadn't changed, but there was a veneer of ice over her words.

"My wife is in this state for a reason. And that is her own fault," Trent observed, then unfolded his arms and placed his palms on his knees. He stared straight ahead again, ignoring the awkward silence which permeated the van.

"I didn't do anything wrong," Adalia protested. "I didn't do anything wrong." She shook her head from side-to-side, denying his anger, and the blame for what'd happened. "I would never do anything to hurt our baby."

"Then how come you did?" Trent countered, eyes flashing from the other side of the van to her face. "You did exactly that and you know it, Adalia. Fuck it, I don't want to talk anymore," he hissed.

The medic shifted back into view, concern written all over her face. "Ma'am? Please face this way. I want you to ignore Mr. Dawson and focus on your breathing."

"Ignore me? I'm her husband!"

"And you're causing her and the baby untold strife by arguing right now. So sit back and shut up," the medic snapped. She brushed a loose strand of shining dark hair back from her eyes and looked down at Adalia with a soft smile. "Focus on your breathing, Mrs. Dawson. Keep your eyes on me."

"I'm not causing stress to anyone," Trent grumbled, but he shut up after that and left Adalia alone.

She'd never believed that he had a side like this, or that he was capable of making her feel small. He'd spent the last year building her up, making her feel like she was really something in his eyes and now… her chest was sore.

The blipping of the monitor behind her head was steady, but man, did her chest hurt. She might die from this pain. Tears sprang up in the corners of her eyes and spilled out, rolling down her cheeks and wetting the back of her head and neck.

"Easy, Adalia," the medic switched to her first name and squeezed her arm gently, "just relax and focus on your breathing and keeping the baby safe. It's going to be alright. We're arriving at the hospital now."

The ambulance slowed to a stop and the back doors were flung open. Cold air rushed in and Adalia's stretcher moved out of those doors. She caught a glimpse of the night sky. They wheeled her through the emergency entrance and into the cool halls of the hospital.

***

It was a private ward because Trent could afford to give his wife, more like his child, a private ward. She gritted her teeth and sat up in the hospital bed, balancing against the pillows.

Her husband stood next to the window, staring out with his arms folded.

Dr. Matheson hadn't been in yet, but the nurses had made it clear she wasn't allowed to go home until he'd checked her out. And even then, she might have to stay for observation.

"This should never have happened," Adalia murmured, stroking the top of her belly and feeling for the baby's movements. She restrained tears, she'd cried enough in the ambulance, and squared her jaw.

"Yeah, it would never have happened if you'd listened to me," Trent grunted. He continued staring out of the window, though he surely couldn't see much down there apart from lights and a few ambulances. It was late.

"Really? Didn't you here the medic? She specifically said you shouldn't stress me out because of the baby."

"It's too late for that Adalia. You've already endangered our child's life by your stubborn insistence on working yourself to the bone." Trent finally looked at her, displaying the anger burning in his gaze. "I warned you about this from the beginning. I fucking warned you, but you wouldn't listen."

"And instead of supporting me right now, you think it's a better idea to scream at me? Is that it? You're the crazy one. You're the selfish one!" Adalia shrieked back at him, the injustice of the situation exploded out of her mouth at last.

She was the one who had to carry a child. And her options were to sit at home while he was out, earning money with Michelle to kiss his ass, or to make a future for herself and a stronger one for the baby.

"You never understood that I wanted to look after you," Trent said, shaking his head. "You've never realized that you can't do it on your own. You can't do it all alone!"

"I can," she barked, "I can and I will and if you continue pushing me about this, I'll make it so that I do everything on my own."

"What the fuck's that supposed to mean?" Trent took two steps towards her, eyebrows jerking up and down, eyes ablaze.

"It means that you don't deserve me if you can treat me like this. What the fuck was that in the ambulance? What's wrong with you?" Adalia placed her palms on the bed and forced herself further upright to glare at the man she loved. "I never thought you were capable of making me feel that way. Like I was baggage. You reminded me of DeShawn."

"Don't ever say that. I'm nothing like that creep," Trent said, raising a finger in warning.

"How could you blame this on me?"

"I asked you to take it easy," he said, lamely. "You've had problems with the baby since three months and you still did what you wanted to do."

"We're never going to agree on this point. But that is no excuse. You should've been there for me when I was in pain. Not shafting me for doing the wrong thing, according to you." Adalia slumped against the pillows again, and a yawn split their argument in two.

Trent's expression softened, the indignation leaked out of his bright blue eyes and his lips relaxed from the tight line. "I'm sorry. That was wrong of me, but I didn't know how else to handle the situation." He cleared his throat. "Do you have any idea how scary that was for me? The thought of losing –"

"Scary for you?!" Adalia growled. "It was scary for you?"

"Am I interrupting?" Matheson poked his head through the door, and gave a sheepish smile.

Adalia wriggled her nose and cast Trent a narrowed-eyed look. "Not at all, Doctor, please come in."

Matheson strode into the private ward and grabbed a clipboard from the end of the bed. He placed it on the adjustable table there and flipped through the pages, checking whatever the hell they kept on doctor's papers. "Everything seems in order here, Adalia. I've checked your progesterone levels and they're still too low, so we're putting you on another course of supplements. Luckily, you're getting close to your due date, so this won't be a problem for much longer."

"How long does she have to stay in hospital?" Trent asked, pulling back the sleeve of his shirt to check the time on his Rolex.

"We'll keep her here for observation for two days... just in case." Matheson smiled at them both. "Is there a problem?"

"I won't be able to stay here for two days," Trent replied, folding his arms. "I've got a business event coming out in a few hours. A shuttle launch and the launch of my company's IPO."

Adalia's mouth went dry. She'd forgotten about that. She'd hoped to stop him from the stupid –

"Perhaps that's for the best," Matheson replied. "Adalia needs as little stress as possible, and I hope I'm not overstepping my bounds here, but from what I saw when I came in, I'd say time apart might be a good idea."

Adalia's cheeks grew hot, and Trent's gaze flashed anger again. He glanced at her then nodded slowly. "I guess you're right. We haven't been behaving ourselves lately."

"Alright, that's settled then. I'm going to send a nurse in with something to help you sleep, Adalia. You need your rest. Try to stop worrying. The key to successfully completing this pregnancy will be lots of bedrest, progesterone and a stress-free environment." Matheson scratched a few notes on the clipboard.

Trent stepped forward. "I'd better get going. I need my sleep for the event tomorrow." He pecked Adalia on the forehead gently. "Call me if there are any problems. Or have the hospital call me."

He marched out of the ward, taking his cell phone out of his pocket and dialing a number as he walked. Michelle, he was probably calling Michelle.

Adalia squeezed her eyes shut and refused to cry.

Chapter Thirteen

"You okay, boss? You don't look so good," Michelle said, standing as close to him as she could without physically making contact.

Trent stared at the shuttle and adjusted his hard hat. "I'm fine. Kindly take a step away from me. I can barely breathe." Everything that'd happened with Adalia was a fucking nightmare.

He'd overreacted, sure, but it'd been for a damn good reason. Trent clenched his fists. He'd warned her over and over again about the dangers of overexerting herself, especially after the doctor had put her on those damn supplements, but she hadn't listened.

Her actions came across as selfish and he couldn't forgive that right now. The sight of her bent over, sweating and crying for help had pushed him to the edge. He'd been incapable of helping her or the baby.

It made him feel like a failure. She'd made his job as protector that much more difficult.

"Mr. Dawson, you need to focus your attention here today," Michelle lectured, grabbing his wrist and placing pressure on it. "Not on your wife."

"Shut up about my wife." Trent paused and moderated his reaction. He turned so that his employee wouldn't see the flush of anger on his cheeks. "Don't overstep your bounds."

"You're right, sir. I'd never want to overstep my boundaries with you. Not too much anyway," she purred, not releasing his arm.

He wrenched it out of her grip and pointed at the shuttle, the men and women scurrying around beneath it. "I suggest you focus on the task at hand. I need everything set up properly before the announcement is made."

"You need to relax, Mr. Dawson," she whispered, trailing her fingertips along the back of his neck, past the collar of his crisply ironed shirt. "Isn't there anything I can do to help you relax?"

"You can get your hands off me for a start," he replied, calmly this time.

The businessman in his tone was clear now. He'd clamped down on his emotions over Adalia and the baby.

Michelle snapped her hand back to her side. "Yes, sir. Is there anything else?"

Trent ignored her question and paced back and forth along the hard pavement. Morning had broken an hour ago and the sunlight glimmered on the point of the shuttle. Crowds gathered in the distance, eager to witness the spectacle.

Trent opened his arms wide to gesture at the masterpiece. And what a fucking masterpiece it was. "The first unmanned flight by the company. If this doesn't get investors chomping at the bit, then I don't know what the hell will."

"It will. This is going to go down in history, sir. You should be proud of yourself," Michelle replied, snapping the straps of her tight shirt.

He narrowed his eyes at her. "Go put a tailored jacket on, Michelle. You look unprofessional."

Michelle gasped and fluttered a hand over her chest, like he'd shot her in the fucking heart or something. She turned and hurried off to fulfil his request.

It was better that way… he could barely concentrate with her around. Not because of latent attraction, no, it was because she annoyed the living shit out of him. Her overpowering perfume was permanently stuck in his nostrils. The only time he didn't smell it was when he was with his wife. The woman who thought a catering business was more important than her pregnancy. Trent clenched his fists again and inhaled deeply. He had to focus!

"Sir?" An engineer, a minor one, not the head engineer, Briggs, tapped him on the arm. "They're asking if you're ready to go or not."

"Oh?" Trent licked his lips. Was he ready for this shit? The speech would come first then they'd launch the shuttle for the world to see. What if it failed?

"Alright, tell them I'll be ready to give the speech in a few minutes. They know when to go?"

"Yes, sir, they know when to – uh – go," the engineer replied, the corners of his lips teasing into an uncomfortable smile.

"Good," Trent replied, nodding. "What are you waiting for?"

The engineer scurried off and Trent pulled a face at the twinge of guilt in his gut. He was on edge this morning alright… blame it on a pregnant wife in danger. But this was it. He could ask himself the same questions. What was he waiting for?

The walk to the podium took fifteen minutes. Fifteen minutes of thinking about everything that had led up to this moment. Months of hard work, away from home and the woman he loved. He'd missed a large portion of Adalia's pregnancy, the ups and downs, because each night he'd gotten home after she'd fallen asleep. Each night he'd drifted off to the sound of her gentle breathing. And each morning he woke up to it and was out the door with a quick kiss on her forehead. He'd been so focussed on getting the IPO out there, making a better future for the baby, that he'd neglected her.

Guilt crippled him on the stairs of the podium, and he had to grip the bannister for a moment to steady himself against it. He rode through waves of regret, listening to the crowds cheer. He'd blamed her for wanting to set up a legacy for their child, but he'd been guilty of the same thing all along. And now she was in the hospital alone and probably seething mad at him for leaving her there when she needed him the most.

Michelle appeared beside him and grabbed his arm under the elbow. "You alright, Mr. Dawson? It's time."

He leaned on her for the briefest moment, then straightened and freed himself from that connection again. "I'm ready."

Trent Dawson mounted the stairs of the podium to announce the IPO for his company, sweat beads sliding down his back, his front, everywhere. Michelle followed him.

***

"I came as soon as I heard, my girl," Sylvester Montclair said, sitting beside her bed in a hospital chair. He kept shifting every few minutes, prodding the flattened cushion underneath his butt, then straightening again.

"I know, Dad. Thanks."

"What happened?" her father asked, doing his cushion prod dance again.

"What didn't happen? That's the more appropriate question." Adalia fluffed her own pillow, using the action to dull her raging nerves. "My progesterone levels are too low and I almost lost the baby thanks to that and doing too much."

"Doing too much? How could you ever do too much?" Sylvester scraped a hand over his greying hair and wrinkled his brow.

They were cut from the same cloth, at least. She believed in hard work because she'd witnesses his stellar work ethic growing up. He'd provided for them, even when he'd had no one else to rely on. A true testament to what a man could do for his family.

Adalia sighed. "I don't want to talk about it, Dad. I can't even think straight right now."

"I thought you said the baby was fine," he said, glancing at the beeping monitor and gauges surrounding her bed. He eyed the IV bag and line attached to her arm with distaste. He'd never been a fan of hospitals. In fact, she couldn't remember a time he'd gone to the doctor, let alone stayed in a hospital bed.

"The baby is fine. But I'm nervous. Trent has this big publicity stunt going on today and I'm terrified it will end badly for him." She picked up the glass of water on her bedside table and glugged some of it down. "We're having a hard enough time as it is already."

Sylvester smacked his lips and considered her in silence.

The ward was decorated in light peach and white linens, the shade reflected on the walls and the dotted curtains which surrounded her bed. It was obviously supposed to be peaceful, but it made her sick to her stomach. She didn't want to be in the hospital while Trent was out there.

"What's the stunt?"

"A shuttle launch. He's going up in a shuttle for the launch of his IPO."

"What?!" Sylvester lurched forward. "That's ridiculous."

"I know, but I figured he knows what he's doing. This is his business and he's spent a long time planning how he wants to take the next step and start gathering investors." Adalia didn't like her defensive tone but she couldn't change it. Even when they disagreed, he was still her husband and she'd stand by him and his choices. Because that was who she was and what a good wife did.

"Girl, you musta lost your damn mind. How could you let that man go?" Sylvester rocked himself out of the chair then kneaded his lower back with arthritic knuckles.

"I can't stop him from doing what he wants." Adalia bit her bottom lip hard, until she tasted blood and her heart rate went up for a few minutes.

A nurse sailed through the door, carrying a tray of food. "What's this? Are you stressing her out, Mr. Montclair?" Nancy had kind eyes and a quick smile, but she didn't extend it to Sylvester.

"I did no such thing." Her father reorganized his sweater vest and met the nurse's gaze head on. "She's got other concerns."

"You'd better shelve those concerns, dear. Your breakfast has arrived and you're supposed to eat it all if you can. Doctor's orders." Nurse Nancy proceeded to check her drip and began changing the IV bag.

"So he's going up while you're in the hospital." Her dad's monotone statement made her heart skip a beat again. Nancy shot him a venomous look. "Any idea when Mr. Billionaire is coming down from the heavens?"

"I didn't ask. It's enough that I'm freaking out about him doing this launch in the first place. I couldn't focus on asking him questions, especially with the pregnancy giving me problems." Adalia encircled the top of her belly with her arms, and imagined hugging her baby for the first time. Only a month and she'd have the little one in her arms. She'd wasted so much time worrying, when she could've been fantasizing about the bright future... or enjoying her pregnancy right now.

Adalia exhaled slowly, puffing her cheeks out. "I don't want it to happen, but he's doing what he has to do. I've always trusted his judgment in the past." She made her voice stern, even though butterflies pounded her from the inside. She couldn't help worrying about this. Trent in a space shuttle. A publicity stunt. What could go wrong?

"It's unacceptable that he'd leave you like this. To do this. Absolutely unacceptable." Sylvester rammed his index finger onto the wooden cabinet beside her bed, and upset the water glass. He picked it up quickly, and avoided looking at Nancy.

"Dad –"

"In fact, I won't stand for it. I'm going to drag that young man right out of that rocket if I have to," Sylvester iterated, then turned on his heel and charged out of the ward.

"What?!" Adalia yelled after him, and images of her father charging at a spacecraft danced through her mind. She couldn't help a grin, it was a funny image, but she didn't need this added pressure. "Dad, you come back here right now!"

Adalia tried to get out of bed, swinging her legs over the side and gripping under her belly. Nurse Nancy forced her back down again, gently.

"No you don't. You're on bedrest and that's that."

Adalia pressed her lips into a thin line. "Fine, but at least give me the remote so I can watch my husband blast off." She twinkled her fingers, though she drowned in her terror on the inside.

Nancy handed her the remote and showed her how to use it, then left.

Adalia aimed the remote at the TV and clicked the *on* button.

Chapter Fourteen

Adalia gripped both sides of her mattress to keep herself sitting straight. She'd never been so afraid in her life. She'd been to hell and back through this pregnancy from the beginning, but this was by far the worst. She stared at the shuttle on the screen.

"And it looks like they're almost ready to launch," the commentator reported, in a deeply serious voice. "What a way to announce the company's IPO, Ted."

"You said it, Bill. This is a moment that'll go down in history for sure."

"The first –"

Adalia muted the TV with a twitch of her finger. She couldn't bear listening to their pretention a second longer. She just wanted to see that stupid shuttle go up in the air and come back down safely. Then she could relax and carry on with her life… and being angry with Trent, of course.

A countdown flashed on the screen and information about the company's IPO in the bottom right hand corner. They were set on ramping up the drama for this then, and it sure worked on her nerves.

"What are you watching?" Nurse Nancy had returned to collect her breakfast tray. She paused and frowned at the cover, which was still over the food.

Adalia was in no mood to even smell the stuff, let alone eat it.

"My husband's shuttle launch. It's a publicity stunt. He's going up to commemorate the announcement of his IPO."

"Oh, I think I heard about that," Nancy replied, absently, "did you eat any of your breakfast, Mrs. Dawson?"

"No," Adalia said, unable to tear her gaze from the TV for even a second. The countdown was in minutes not seconds, but once they hit the minute mark, it would probably switch to a second counter.

Would there be a cinematic BLAST OFF flashing on the screen? God, she could barely think straight.

"You need to keep your strength up. Perhaps you should turn that TV off," the nurse suggested, drawing closer with her palm flat and pointing in Adalia's direction.

"Over my dead body," Adalia replied, slapping the remote against her chest to guard it, still not removing her gaze from the TV screen. Two minutes to go. What was Trent doing on board? Was Michelle with him?

This entire thing was absurd.

"Mrs. Dawson, the doctor said you shouldn't –"

"I don't care what the doctor said," Adalia growled and readjusted herself against the pillows.

"Mrs. Dawson, it's imperative you don't stress yourself out."

Her gaze was glued to the screen, but Nancy's constant whining had given her a headache. "Do you know what's stressing me out? You telling me I'm going to get stressed out. So, either sit down to watch the shuttle launch with me, or disappear back to wherever it is you nurse's hang out when you're not giving me trouble."

Nancy made a few huffing noises, then sidled over and sat down in the visitor's chair.

Adalia sighed. It made her feel better to have someone there with her. Anyway, her dad would surely head back soon… he had to know he couldn't stop a shuttle launch. The countdown hit the minute mark and Adalia's pulse quickened.

Nancy reached over and squeezed her hand gently. "Relax, Adalia. He's going to be fine." That was the first time the nurse had used her first name and it only made Adalia more nervous.

"Thirty seconds to go," she murmured, gripping Nancy's hand and squeezing so hard it had to hurt. The nurse didn't complain or pull away. The shuttle vibrated with energy, things were about to get serious. She couldn't bring herself to turn on the commentary and up the tension.

The countdown hit ten seconds and her stomach clenched tight. This was it. Trent was about to take off into the atmosphere.

"Here we go, this is it," Adalia whispered.

"What a great moment," Nancy said, her voice forced.

BLAST OFF!

The words flashed on the screen and the shuttle's thrusters kicked in. Flames spat from their ends and the craft was propelled into the blue, soaring towards the stratosphere.

"Oh God, this is terrifying," Adalia said, grasping her belly at a twinge of pain. "I have a bad feeling about it."

The craft was high above the launch pad. There was a ripple of light, and explosion, and a ball of flame engulfed the craft. Bits of it flew off in every direction, scattering like the arms of a fireworks display on the fourth of July.

"What? What just –?" Adalia swallowed. "No, that can't be."

Nancy reached for the remote and tried to jerk it from her hand. Adalia clung to it, eyes wide and stomach tying itself into knots.

"No, no, no, this isn't right. That didn't happen."

The camera zoomed in on the sky, where bits of the dead shuttle streaked across it, trailing smoke.

"No, I don't believe it. Trent was in there. Trent was in that shuttle." Adalia repeated. "I won't believe it."

Nancy finally wrenched the control from her grasp and switched the TV off. "Calm down, you need to stay calm."

"Calm? Why? Calm." She couldn't string a sentence together. Couldn't believe it. It was a sick joke, it had to be. That couldn't have been her husband up there. It couldn't have been. "Trent. I want him to come back."

Her abdomen exploded in pain and contracted around the baby. Adalia screamed and gripped her belly. The monitors behind her went crazy.

Nurse Nancy darted from the room and Adalia was left in agony. Trent was gone and the baby… what was this? Another wave of pain, ripples spread through her tightening and releasing, the worst spasm ever felt.

"She's gone into labor, Doctor," Nancy said, hustling Dr. Matheson into the room.

"Adalia," he said, grasping her chin. "Adalia, you need to focus on me. The baby is in distress. We need to get the baby out now. Do you understand?"

Her body was a nerve-ending. She stared at the doctor. "Trent."

"I'm sorry, Adalia, but you have to focus on the baby. If we don't get it out now…" he trailed off.

Another contraction hit, and she threw back her head and screamed at the ceiling.

***

Trent walked down the stairs of the podium, ignoring the swell of excitement from the crowd. The shuttled had just taken off, screaming to the sky, the first unmanned flight for the company, but he couldn't focus on it. He couldn't think of anything other than Adalia.

"Mr. Dawson," Michelle called out behind him, over the cheering crowd. "Trent! Where are you going?" She caught up and walked beside him, a giraffe clip-clopping in her high heels.

"Where I belong."

"But you belong here," Michelle said. "Come on, sir, we have to take advantage of the momentum on this. I'll help you." She flashed him her sluttiest smile, she licked her bottom lip, which was coated in bright red lipstick.

"Enough, Michelle. Enough of your bullshit!" he yelled, and a couple of passers-by shifted their gazes from the trailing smoke from the shuttle take-off, the event he'd worked on for seven months, to their petty argument. "I will never want you. Do you understand that? I will never want to be with you in any capacity.

And if it weren't for your father, you wouldn't even have a job right now."

"Trent, stop it. I don't like it when you talk like that. It's crazy," Michelle replied then grabbed his sleeve.

Trent ripped it from her and turned, opening his mouth to give the woman a piece of his mind.

Screams broke out from the pavilion and he paused, glancing back at the crowd. Most of them were on their feet, pointing at the sky or gripping their cheeks in shock. Trent followed the stares and blinked once.

The shuttle had exploded.

"Okay, now you definitely can't leave." Michelle said, glaring up at the worst omen possible for the release of the company's IPO.

"Fuck it," Trent said, "I've got something more important to attend to." He hurried off, away from the crowd of engineers rushing towards him, the shocked stares of spectators, and particularly away from Michelle.

"More important than the business?!" she yelled after him. He didn't bother answering her.

Trent made for his car, whipping out his phone to check for messages. It buzzed to life in his hand, and he jumped. Unknown number.

"Yes?"

"Mr. Dawson?" A woman asked, and the timbre of her voice gave him shivers. Not the good kind that his wife gave him, the kind he'd get when someone walked over his grave.

"This is Trent, what do you want?"

"I'm calling with news about your wife, sir. She's just gone into premature labor. Dr.Matheson requested your presence at the hospital as soon as you're able."

"I'm on my way," he grunted, and his insides felt like it turned to scrambled eggs. He shoved his phone back into his pocket and ran for the car, heart racing. He'd left her there all alone, to fend for herself, and this had happened.

How was it possible? She'd been fine when he left her. Sure, they'd fought, but she'd been in a stable condition. The doctor had her on those progesterone supplements. Nothing could've happened to cause this.

"Shit, shit, shit," he growled, grabbing his keys out of his pocket. He reached the lot and ran to his Audi, muscles wound tight. The red car waited for him, sleek and calm beneath the morning sun.

"Boy!" a man shouted nearby.

Trent halted and looked around, then did a double-take. Sylvester Montclair charged across the parking lot, glaring at him. The old man wasn't frail this time, but full of vigor for a seventy-something year old.

"Mr. Montclair, I don't have time to talk right now, Adalia –"

"Adalia is in the hospital alone because of your cock-brained idea to be here." Sylvester paused and looked up at the sky, then frowned. "Wait a second." His gaze traced the lines of smoke streaking the sky. "What happened?"

"The shuttle exploded," Trent shrugged then inched towards the car door, extending his keys.

"No," Sylvester whispered, "no. Adalia thinks you're in that shuttle."

Trent stopped again, dropped his hand to his side. "What are you talking about?"

"Adalia thinks you were meant to go up in that shuttle. She probably watched the launch on the news. Saw that thing explode."

"And she thinks I'm on board." The blood drained from his face and he clenched the keys so hard, they bit into the palm of his hand. That was probably what had driven her over the edge.

She'd stressed hard enough to induce labor. He'd worried about her endangering their baby through her working so hard, then promptly stressed her out to the point that their baby was about to be born prematurely.

"She's in labor," Trent said, and the world moved beneath him. The ground rushed up to meet him then halted.

Sylvester had caught him as he fell. "Easy, boy, let's go. We'll go together. It's going to be fine."

"This is my fault," he croaked, keys dangling from his fingertips. He straightened slowly then rearranged his shirt.

"Now's not the time for blame. It's the time for action." Sylvester's expression softened and he took the keys from Trent as they approached his car. "How do you work this thing?"

Trent managed a smile, though his mind was aflame. He'd done this to her, he was the one who'd endangered their child. A memory, plucked from his darkest moment, flashed in front of his eyes.

Sitting in the back of the ambulance, while she cried because of what he'd said. Not because of the pain of the baby, or fear, but because he'd made her feel worse about it when he should've supported her.

Trent tensed and took the keys back. "I'll drive."

Chapter Fifteen

"I need to see my wife. Now!" Trent stood in front of reception, while Sylvester Montclair paced up and down behind him. "She's with Dr. Matheson. Adalia Dawson." He was out of breath. The drive over had been high speed, and neither of them had enjoyed a second of it.

The receptionist, her name tag read Molly, took her sweet time flipping through information on a few pages, then turned to the computer and typed in Adalia's details. She chewed on the end of a pen and sniffed. "I'm sorry sir, but she's in labor. You won't be able to see her until it's over."

"What?! Why the hell not? I literally received a message from this hospital which said the doctor requested my fucking presence! Why can't I see my wife?"

"Sir, please calm down –"

"This is unacceptable," Sylvester put in, stepping forward and slamming both fists onto the desk. "She's my daughter and his wife. Take us to her, this instant."

"Sir, I'm afraid –"

"If you don't take me to her I'm going to tear shit up," Trent said, raising a finger at Molly. He didn't glance at Sylvester, but the old man had his back for sure. Adalia needed them, and Trent intended on being there for her for the rest of their lives. "Which room is she in?" He waggled his index finger under her nose and she tried to stare at it, crossing her eyes in the effort.

"What's going on here?" A nurse stepped into view, carrying a clipboard and a frown. "Are these gentlemen giving you trouble, Molly?" The nurse glanced over her shoulder for security.

"Yes, we're giving her trouble," Trent replied, "and I'll give you trouble too if you don't get me to Adalia Dawson this second."

"Adalia," the nurse's eyes widened. "Are you Trent? Are you Mr. Dawson?"

"Yes," he studied her expression. The nurse's entire face had gone pale.

She looked back at Molly and shook her head slightly. "I'll handle this, Molly. Get on with your work."

The nurse swept forward, hand outstretched. "Mr. Dawson, I'm Nancy. I was with your wife when she went into labor. She thought, well, honestly, she thought you were on the shuttle when it exploded and it –" Nancy broke off and looked past his shoulder. "Mr. Montclair, I didn't see you there."

Trent still hadn't taken her hand, so she extended it to Adalia's father instead. Sylvester shook it and gave her a warm smile. "We're looking for Adalia. Do you know what room she's in?"

Nancy focused on him then switched her gaze back to Trent. "I'm sorry to be the bearer of bad news, but the baby was in distress. Dr. Matheson rushed her into the operating room for an emergency C-section."

Trent's bubble popped. The lobby wasn't a room anymore. It was a vacuum, filled with people and things which he couldn't see. This was his fault. Both of them were in grave danger because he'd left her, because he'd fought with her. The rhetoric tortured him, rubbing salt into his wounds.

"Mr. Dawson?" Nancy grabbed him under one elbow and Sylvester took the other. Together, they walked him to a chair in the corner and sat him down. The nurse bent down and placed a hand on his shoulder, then peered into his eyes. "Mr. Dawson, can you hear me?"

He nodded slowly then swallowed a dry gulp. "I'm here. I mean, I can hear you. Is she okay?"

"She's stable and cognizant of what's going on," Nancy replied, then clicked her fingers over her shoulder at someone. "Get him a glass of water, please, and take him through to maternity." She turned back to him. "That's where they'll take her once the baby's been delivered."

"The baby," he said. God, his child would be born today, premature. "Is the baby going to be alright?"

"I can't say yet, Mr. Dawson. I haven't been in to see what's going on, but as soon as I know, you'll know, alright? You need to come with me now." Nancy rose and Sylvester helped Trent to his feet.

For the second time in the span of an hour, Trent pulled himself together and checked that his clothes were straight. He had to be stronger than this, but this moment was the most terrifying.

He'd never felt this out of control of his future. The two people that he loved were both in the same room and he couldn't be with them.

Nancy waved over another orderly. "This is George. He'll take you through to maternity," she said, and gave Trent a glass of water. "Try to keep calm, Mr. Dawson. I know this is a difficult time, but you'll make it through. I'm sure your wife and child will be fine."

"Please, find out what's going on. I have to know," Trent replied, and it came out like a plea, because that was what it was. Nancy gave a grave nod then disappeared off down the hall, gliding on the linoleum like an angel.

"Let's go," Sylvester prodded.

Trent followed George through the halls of the hospital, mind on nothing but his wife, on the thought of seeing her alive and well, with a baby in her arms. He couldn't live without her, and that meant the universe or God, or whoever had pulled this sick joke couldn't take her away from him.

"Trent," Sylvester grumbled, "she's going to be okay. Keep it together."

The words slid off him like water off a duck's back. He was as together as he could be right now. The orderly walked them into maternity and everything green became pink instead.

They turned a corner and strode into a private ward.

Adalia lay in the bed on her back, breathing lightly, with her gaze trained on the window. Tears streamed down her cheeks and she gripped the blanket in her fist.

"Adalia," he whispered. "Adalia, oh my God."

She turned her head, and her expression flickered from agony to wonder.

"Trent?"

***

"Trent," she whispered, and flopped her arms at him, like she couldn't use them.

He rushed to her side and gathered her head in his arms, then planted a soft kiss on her skin. She was covered in a thin sheen of sweat, but he could've lapped it up. She was alive. His wife was alive, in spite of all that had happened.

"I thought you were dead," she croaked.

"It was an unmanned flight, my love. I would never go up with you pregnant, waiting here. What do you think I am?"

"You were so angry," she whispered, eyes brimming with tears. "I thought you'd leave me."

"Never," he replied, fiercely. Guilt wormed a hole through his chest, and he bent over her again, planting soft wet kisses all over her face, every inch of skin he could reach. "Never. I will never leave you."

He looked back for Sylvester, but the old man was gone. He'd probably figured this was a personal moment and Trent was grateful for that. He'd broken down enough in front of Adalia's father.

"I'm so glad you're okay," he said, then finally sat down on the edge of the bed, holding her hand. "I was worried sick."

"I'm sorry for everything," she replied. "I should've listened to you."

"Don't," he said, pressing a finger to her lips. "We've both made mistakes, and done the best we can. All that matters is that we're together now."

Adalia squeezed his hand and her eyes drifted shut for a moment then opened again.

"The baby, Adalia. Is the baby alright?"

"He was when I gave birth. That's what they told me. They're going to bring him in soon," Adalia whispered, then shut her eyes again. She was obviously exhausted, but she was safe.

And Trent had a son. His heart grew in size at the thought. A *son*, his own son and Adalia was safe. Somehow it'd worked out. Somehow, everything was fine, just like Sylvester had said.

The door to the ward swung inward. Nancy strolled in, holding a blue-wrapped bundle in her arms and wearing a grin which lit the entire room. Her feet whispered along the floor and she stopped beside the bed, rocking the baby gently.

"It's time for you to hold him, Adalia, and to feed him if you can." Nancy took the blanket off the tiny baby, too small for Trent's liking, and handed him to his mother.

He was perfect… ten toes and ten fingers. Trent exhaled slowly, the pressure in his chest grew and swelled until it filled him from his brain down to his toes. That was his child.

Tears spilled from his eyes and hit the bedsheets. Adalia stripped her hospital gown open and laid the child against her bare breasts, with tender care. She cried too, but with a smile on her face.

"Can she sit up?"

"Not yet," Nancy replied, "she has to stay supine for at least eight hours to speed the healing process. Dealing with a C-section is a more complicated process, both during and after."

"Alright," he said then cleared his throat. "Mind giving us some time alone? As a family." He loved that. By far the best sentence that'd ever been uttered.

"Of course," Nancy rose, and walked to the door, then looked back once, as if to appreciate them standing together. She shut the door behind her with a gentle click.

"He's so perfect," Trent mused, immediately. "Small, but perfect."

"He'll get bigger," Adalia replied fondly. "He'll get bigger and stronger and be our little man in no time." She giggled and the baby made a crooning noise of complaint, searching for the nipple again. She helped the baby latch then looked up at him, dazed. "What will we call him, my love?"

Trent reached between the skin of her breast and the baby's, and stuck his finger in his little palm. The baby grabbed hold and didn't let go. Trent's eyes filled with tears again, but he held them back.

"He looks like an Isaac," he murmured, then met Adalia's gaze for approval.

"Isaac," she repeated. "I like that. It's got spunk." She ran her finger down his creamy brown cheek and rested it on his button nose. "Hello, little Isaac. Welcome to the world. Meet your daddy."

"Shouldn't he be in an incubator?" Trent asked, and searched the room for the equipment.

"It's in another room. But the doctor said that having him close to me will work too. It's a method that's being used more these days. It's natural." Adalia grinned, her first true smile in what seemed like a year. In fact, it was a half a year since he'd seen her grinning like nothing was wrong.

"I'm so happy," he said. Because his wife was happy, his son was safe and everything in the world was finally right again.

"Me too." She grabbed his free hand and squeezed the fingertips. "We did it, Trent, we're parents."

"Now the hard part starts," he quipped.

Adalia gave a soft chuckle and readjusted Isaac on her breast.

The door to the room opened and Dr. Matheson swept in, carrying nothing but a frown. "I'm glad to see you here, Mr. Dawson. I was worried you wouldn't make it in time for the birth."

"I arrived just after, unfortunately," Trent said, "but in time to name our son, Isaac."

"That's a strong name," the doctor replied, then took a deep breath. "I have some news," he said, then paused and picked up the clipboard off the end of the bed. "I need both of you to remain seated and calm, please."

Trent's stomach did a turn. "What is it, doc? We don't need any bad news right now. I think my business might've just fallen through the floor."

Matheson gave two swift coughs then straightened. "I'm sorry to tell you this, but Isaac is gravely ill."

"No," Adalia murmured, and tightened her grip on their child.

-To be continued in Book 4-

If you enjoyed this title, I would appreciate your leaving a review of the book. Good reviews encourage an author to write as well as help books to sell. Good reviews can be just a few short sentences describing what you liked about the book without having a spoiler. If you could spend 30 seconds writing a review, I would appreciate it: you can review this title right now at your favorite retailer.

Here is a preview of the **next book** you may also enjoy:

Love Everlasting: Tenacious Billionaire BWWM Romance Series, Book 4

"**WHAT DID** you say?" Adalia adjusted her son, her gorgeous little Isaac, on her breast and stared at Dr. Matheson as if he'd grown an extra head.

Trent's hand gripped her shoulder, fingernails digging into the flesh. She glanced up at him but he didn't meet her gaze… he was slack-jawed, cheeks pale.

Dr. Matheson heaved a sigh and Adalia shifted her focus back to him, holding Isaac close, appreciating the smell of his tan skin and the gentle suckling noises he made as he fed.

"I'm afraid that your son is ill." Matheson cleared his throat. "Please, Mr. Dawson, take a seat."

Trent seemed resistant to the idea – his grip on her shoulder trembled for a few seconds – but he sank to the chair beside her bed, slipping his hand down to rest on her forearm.

"He's ill…" Adalia repeated, stroking a finger over Isaac's forehead. "He can't be ill. He's perfect."

"This is going to be difficult for you to hear, Mrs. Dawson. Perhaps one of the nurses can take Isaac for a rest while we discuss it."

A nurse bustled through the doors at the end of the ward on cue, smiling with a pity smile. Trent went rigid beside her bed and shuddered again. "You will not touch my son," he growled at her.

"Trent," Adalia whispered. "Relax. Let's hear what the doctor has to say." She had to remain calm for her son's sake. She wouldn't risk upsetting him, even though her insides were knotted with anxiety.

Dr. Matheson worked his jaw, trying to articulate but failing. The nurse stayed by the door, gaze darkening thanks to Trent's snappy comment. She folded her arms and looked to Matheson for guidance, as if he could override the father's wishes. *Stupid bitch.*

"Spit it out," Trent said.

Matheson jerked and readjusted his white coat. "Isaac has an abnormally high white blood cell count. Conversely, his red blood cell count is low. We need to perform a biopsy to ascertain exactly what these results mean."

"What are the possibilities?" Adalia asked, arms pulling her son closer still. He suckled and smacked his lips, then popped off her breast, falling fast asleep. She covered her chest absentmindedly.

"Cancer. Leukemia specifically." Matheson showed them his palms at the exact moment Trent leapt to his feet. "But we need to do the tests first."

"What else could it be? What else?"

"An autoimmune deficiency, but that's highly unlikely. He doesn't have any rashes and hasn't had seizures." Matheson flipped the file open to study the paperwork again, but it was obviously his method of avoiding their shocked gazes.

Panic gathered in the center of Adalia's chest, a leaden ball which threatened to drop through her and drag tears down her cheeks. She welled up and used one hand to dab beneath her eyes. She didn't want to cry with Matheson and the nurse in the room.

"So you're telling us it can only be leukemia."

"It's the most likely outcome," Matheson conceded. "I'm sure you understand this is a serious prognosis and should it be confirmed, we'll have to deal with it accordingly."

"What are our options?" Adalia asked, swallowing to stop the tears. She swallowed and swallowed but the lump in her throat wouldn't go away. She looked at Trent. His face was lined with anger, his go-to reaction when he couldn't deal.

"I'd much rather discuss that after we have confirmed the prognosis."

"You'll tell us now," Trent commanded. "You will tell us right now, Dr. Matheson, otherwise you will kindly explain why you brought this up prior to ascertaining whether Isaac has leukemia or not."

"Calm down," Adalia murmured. Tears spilled from her eyes. "Just calm down."

Matheson stared at them, opening and closing his mouth again. "There's a new therapy which could successfully cure Isaac should he have leukemia."

"What is it?" Adalia asked immediately, trying but failing to rid herself of the tears. "We'll do anything."

"We managed to preserve some of Isaac's stem cells, found in the umbilical cord. Simply put, the treatment involves an injection of these stem cells into Isaac's bone marrow."

"Then let's do that. We'll do that," Trent said, settling back as if the matter was dealt with. Her husband was all bravado and self-belief, but the fear coursed behind his façade. If it wasn't anger protecting him, it was the business-like confidence.

Little Isaac mewled once and went back to sleep, sucking on thin air with his curved lips parted. Her precious baby. She couldn't let anything happen to him. She would rather die. She would trade her life for his in a heartbeat.

"It's an exceptionally expensive treatment on the frontier of cancer research, Mr. Dawson." Matheson delivered the blow in a lowered voice, a croaking whisper which the sullen nurse wouldn't be able to overhear.

"And so? I'm a billionaire. I think we'll be okay." Trent tried to reassure the others but his shoulders had dropped. Space Inc. had taken a hit because of the shuttle explosion, hopefully not too big of a hit. Trent had invested more than just his time in getting that craft into the air.

"Do I have your permission to proceed with the test?"

"Will it be painful for him?" Adalia clutched the baby to her chest again, shifting him so that he was vertical with his head resting below her collar bone.

"There will be a certain level of pain involved."

The nurse stepped forward from her spot beside the door and Adalia gripped Isaac tighter. She gave the woman a warning look, gritting her teeth.

"Please, Mrs. Dawson, this is the only way to know for sure." Matheson gave her a warm smile, encouraging, but it didn't make a damn difference to her. She didn't want to give her baby up to anyone, least of all the nurse with the eager stare.

"Adalia," Trent said, rising beside her. "Give Isaac to me." He took the baby from her carefully, holding him like precious cargo, and walked over to the nurse.

The nurse took Isaac and he woke in her arms. He kicked his little legs, waved his fists in the air, struggling to be free of his receiving blanket. Isaac cried, two sharp wails which turned into a full-blown bawl.

"Give him back," Adalia said, the tears coming again, racking her body. She sobbed, watching helplessly as the nurse took her screaming son and walked out of the room. "I need him close to me. Bring back my baby!"

Trent rushed to her side and wrapped his arms around, resting his head on her shoulder. "It's okay, honey, it's going to be okay. We'll make him better."

"I'll leave you two alone," Dr. Matheson said. "I'm so sorry, Mr. and Mrs. Dawson." He tipped his head and walked for the door with short steps.

Trent rocked Adalia backwards and forwards, soothing her with subtle coos and words. "We have the money to make this happen. Isaac is going to be okay."

How could he possibly know that?

Adalia couldn't speak. She couldn't think. All she could process were Isaac's distant cries which rang in her ears, driving her deeper and deeper into despair.

If you enjoyed this sample then look for **Love Everlasting: Tenacious Billionaire BWWM Romance Series, Book 4**.

Here is a preview of **another book** you may also enjoy:

OVER THE last few months, Alexa barely managed to keep her life in order. She had started dating Jerome more seriously, but it did not stop her from having feelings for William. Unfortunately, days like today were impossible to avoid. When she first started working as a publicist for William, she expected to collect a tidy sum. What she did not expect was the impossibility of acting normal around someone she was so attracted to. She sighed.

Across the room, William looked up. "What's the matter? I thought you said everything was about to be under control."

Alexa shook her head. "No, everything is fine. I was thinking about something I need to get done around the house," she lied.

William stood up and walked across the room. From behind her, he leaned in closer as he looked over the press releases she was working on. At this close range, she felt the sexual attraction oozing from his body. He ran his fingers through his hair and Alexa wished his hand was hers. She chided to herself... this was ridiculous. Everything was going so well with Jerome. If she wanted to stay faithful, she would need to leave now.

Abruptly, she stood up and shut the laptop screen. She turned around to come face-to-face with William. He waited for her to say something that could explain her sudden movement. At this close range, she could kiss him if she wanted to. His lips were so close to hers...

"I need to leave," she explained as she tried to fumble with the zipper on her backpack. "I will send you the finished press releases later tonight. We should be able to finish this over e-mail or the phone."

Confused, William nodded. He had no clue why she was acting so strange. Although he knew she had a boyfriend now, he never did anything to imply any non-chivalrous intent. "That's fine. Just send it to my personal e-mail account. If I don't answer right away, shoot me a text message and I'll get to it right away."

***

After driving around for a while, Alexa was able calm down enough to go home. She was taken. No matter what happened, she had to remember that fact. As she entered the apartment, she repeated this basic fact over and over in her mind. It did not matter. Despite her best efforts, the very thought of William aroused her.

Glancing at the clock, Alexa decided she could give in to her urges just this once. She would go home, run a bath and spend some time fantasizing about William. Having fantasies about him was not out of the question. Plenty of women fantasized about other men without acting on them. She frowned.

A sudden vibration surprised her. Reaching down, she realized her phone was buzzing. It was William.

Flipping to the message with her fingers, she tried to read what it said while she pulled into the garage.

You left only moments ago, but I miss you already. I think I may have sent off the press release by mistake.

She groaned. Despite the cuteness of his message, William created additional work for her. Shaking her head, she messaged him back.

Don't touch anything. I'll fix it on Friday. :).

Exiting the car, Alexa climbed the stairs to her apartment. She unlocked the door and threw off her purse. Finally, she was home. Wandering into the kitchen, she poured herself a glass of wine. This would be perfect. She would start with a glass of wine, fill the tub and relax.

Turning around, Alexa dropped her wine glass. Standing in front of her was Jerome. Her mouth fell open as she tried to think of what to say.

Jerome shuffled his feet in an awkward manner. Now that she arrived home, he felt bashful and did not know what to say. Pulling the flowers out from behind his back, he held them out to Alexa. "I thought I would surprise you," he whispered as he gave her a hopeful smile.

Alexa grinned. "This is so sweet. What's the occasion?" she asked.

He shrugged. "I figured you needed something to brighten your day. You've been working with that one client so much lately that I never see you."

Alexa felt a pain in her heart. He had waited for her with the intention of surprising her. Jerome was so sweet and she had spent the last few minutes fantasizing about William. Smiling, she took the flowers and tried to hide her guilty expression. "That's amazing. It's supposed to be over by Friday, so I'll have some extra time to spend with you, Jerome."

If you enjoyed this sample then look for **Love Renewed - Fervent Billionaire BWWM Romance Series, Book 3**.

Here is a preview of **another story** you may enjoy:

Love Abided: Audacious Billionaire BWWM Romance Series, Book 3

IT HAS been three weeks since the marriage proposal and Chante knew what she had to do. She knew it since the night she said 'yes' to Dr. Leo Cadman. Her sense of right and wrong had been bothering her like crazy since. It wasn't like she didn't have feelings for Leo. In her heart there was a special place for him. Even her common sense was telling her she did the right thing in accepting the ring. But how could she deny the little nagging voice telling her she was a fraud?

If it were just her and Leo in the equation, the conclusion would be a given. There was no doubt that he was the perfect man for her. She could learn to love him totally. But the existence of one Jared Lowell made the equation more complex than it should have been.

Considering that Jared hasn't even hinted about his true feelings- or any feeling for that matter- about her, Chante thought she was awfully stupid to feel guilty about accepting Leo's marriage proposal.

Couldn't she just consider Jared an infatuation and move on with her 'happily ever after' with an eligible doctor who obviously was crazy in love with her?

She knew the answer. If she was really honest with herself, she knew it all along. It wasn't like a bolt of lightning that just came out of the blue. She was in love with Jared and she had to tell Leo the truth. Whatever the consequences or outcome about her decision, she had to do it soon.

The engagement ring he had given her lay heavily in her left hand ring finger. She shouldn't even have worn it out onto the streets. The single solitaire diamond reflected the light from the street lamps she passed by.

She spotted a small café, entered the premises and sat at a barstool. The bar of the café faced a glass mirror looking out into the street. It was a small dive compared to the more glitzy ones but it was in Queens and near the home she shared with her brother, Markey. His sleeping meds had taken effect almost immediately and Chante took the time to go out into the fresh air and think about her dilemma.

Droplets of rain cascaded down the glass window as Chante let out a sigh of frustration.

"Swell…" she muttered under her breath.

Even the weather was a reflection of the guilt in her heart. It was a good thing Leo was gone for the entire week. He had to attend a medical conference in Atlanta, giving Chante precious time to work out how she would handle the situation when he came back. Initially he was hesitant to leave so soon after the proposal. He wanted to spend as much time as he could with her but Chante reassured him it was fine. The medical conference was a step forward in his career as an ER doctor.

But even Chante understood why she wanted him away. It would give her time to put her thoughts into perspective and she could only do that if she wasn't feeling so guilty about him being around her all the time.

She had to break the engagement. It wasn't fair to the guy. How could she pretend to love him when she knew that her feelings didn't go deep enough to deserve the ring he had given her?

And Jared was gone too. He left word that he would be gone for a few days to attend to some personal concerns. That left Chante feeling gloomy and abandoned, but also relieved that he didn't have to know about her current status – engaged to Dr. Leo Cadman.

She was hoping that by the time Jared got back, if he ever came back at all, she would have untangled herself from this farce of an engagement.

Right now, she felt trapped between a rock and a hard place, but one thing was for sure, she had to break an engagement that she was sure she couldn't live up to.

She probably would end up alone and miserable just the same, but at least her conscience wouldn't be nagging her day and night.

Chante ordered a beer and nursed her drink. She glanced at her watch and decided to drink up and head for home. The rain was now just a drizzle and she could sprint the few blocks home.

She pulled out her purse to pay the bill when a familiar voice greeted her.

"Well-well-well, if it isn't my favorite girl. Fancy meeting you here." The voice sneered.

Chante whirled swiftly around, a sudden fear creeping into her heart. She knew that voice.

"Oh… hi Jimmy…" Chante addressed him with a squeaky voice.

The new arrival was Jimmy Derollo, her ex-boyfriend. The guy always gave her the creeps. Chante wondered what she ever saw in him. Even now as he sidled towards her in the bar, she felt her skin crawl and the hair on the back of her neck stand on end.

Their last confrontation weeks ago on the sidewalk while waiting for the bus was something Chante wanted to forget. The hard slap she gave him on the face after he tried to kiss her still resounded in her ear. She vaguely remembered the threat he made as she swiftly boarded the bus. But she couldn't forget the murderous look in his eyes as the bus pulled away from him.

The bar was half-full and Chante knew that Jimmy wouldn't try anything stupid. One scream and even the bartender would probably come to her rescue. Still…she wasn't sure if she could deal with him once she was outside the confines of the bar. He could follow her home and she came alone.

If you enjoyed this sample then look for **Love Abided: Audacious Billionaire BWWM Romance Series, Book 3.**

Other Books by Shyla Starr

- Persuasive Billionaire BWWM Romance Series

- Elusive Billionaire Romance Series

- Lonely Billionaire Romance Series

- Ardent Billionaire Romance Series

- Fervent Billionaire BWWM Romance Series

- Audacious Billionaire BWWM Romance Series

Get the latest update on new releases from the author at:

https://shylastarr.com/newsletter/

About the Author - Shyla Starr

Shyla currently specializes in writing interracial romance stories and is a huge fan of the alpha male. Simply put, there just aren't enough stories about mixed couple romances, which is something she is aiming to fix.

Being a bookworm all her life, when Shyla discovered men she also realized how easy it was to fulfill her fantasies through her writing.

When not writing and fantasizing about men, Shyla enjoys dancing, reading and chilling with her friends.

Connect with Shyla Starr

I really appreciate you reading my book! Here are my social media coordinates:

Friend me on Facebook:
https://www.facebook.com/shylastarrauthor

Follow me on Twitter: https://twitter.com/shylstarr

Check me out on Goodreads:
https://www.goodreads.com/author/show/8436084.Shyla_Starr

Subscribe to my newsletter:
https://shylastarr.com/newsletter/

Visit my website: https://shylastarr.com/

9 781988 083803